"This can't be an earthquake," Sierra told herself, her thoughts shrieking too loudly inside her skull.

Earthquakes sometimes rattled the windows a little or shook the dishes in the cupboard for a second or two. This had to be something else entirely. The chandelier was swinging in a wide circle, almost brushing the ceiling. She struggled to get to her feet and fell again, grasping at the corner of the entryway carpet in a panicked attempt to steady herself.

The young man was suddenly beside her. He pulled her up into a sitting position and they held each other, managing together to stay at least this much upright. Then—as suddenly as it had begun—the shaking stopped.

Sierra realized that she had closed her eyes; she opened them to find herself pressed against his chest like a frightened child. She leaned back, staring into his eyes.

"Are you all right?"

"Yes." She nodded, slowly, wondering if it was true.

Then the earth buckled and snapped beneath the building, and the nightmare began again.

Look for these historical romance titles
from Archway Paperbacks.

Hindenburg, 1937 by Cameron Dokey
San Francisco Earthquake, 1906 by Kathleen Duey
Great Chicago Fire, 1871 by Elizabeth Massie (coming soon)

San Francisco
Earthquake
1906

Kathleen Duey

AN ARCHWAY PAPERBACK
Published by POCKET BOOKS
New York London Toronto Sydney Tokyo Singapore

AN ARCHWAY PAPERBACK *Original*

An Archway Paperback published by
POCKET BOOKS, a division of Simon & Schuster Inc.
1230 Avenue of the Americas, New York, NY 10020

ISBN: 0-671-03602-5

First Archway Paperback printing September 1999

10 9 8 7 6 5 4 3 2 1

AN ARCHWAY PAPERBACK and colophon are registered trademarks of Simon & Schuster Inc.

Front cover illustration by Sandy Young/Studio Y

Printed in the U.S.A.

IL 7+

For Karen A. Bale
Truest of friends

E San Francisco Francisco

Earthquake

1906

1

The sound of the northbound's whistle woke Sierra O'Neille. Staring into the darkness, she took a few seconds to remember why this was an important day. When she did, she shivered and pulled up her blanket. Mrs. Evans had given it to her. It was old and patched, but the thick wool was still warm.

The train whistle came again, louder. Sierra could picture the long dark cars of the Central Pacific freight train clattering around the curve below the Channels Street station. Pulling the blanket up to cover her face, she waited, listening. A third hollow whistle-shriek came a minute later, fading into the fierce rhythm of the steam engine as the train rolled north toward Napa.

Sierra held still, trying not to think about Cameron. She breathed slowly, straining to hear the first of the Chinese lily wagons. There it was. Right on time, as always. Wheels creaking over the soft, whuffling breath of the horses, it passed beneath her window, bringing the flowers in from the fields.

Sierra sighed at the first muffled crow of Mrs. Evans's rooster, shut up in the coop behind the boardinghouse. Then she stretched. This was the daily combination of sounds that meant it was almost 4:00—about an hour before sunup—and time for her to rise.

She sat up and swung her feet to the chilly floor. Her thin muslin nightgown did nothing to block the damp cool of the morning, and she knew without looking that it was foggy. March mornings in San Francisco always were.

Sierra pushed her hair back over her shoulders, then struck a lucifer and turned up the gas in her wall lamp. The flame flickered, then bounced into life, the wick emitting an acrid scent. She turned the flow of gas down until the flame was low, giving off just enough light so she could get ready for work. Mrs. Evans paid their water and sewage costs, but the gas bills were divvied up among the boarders.

Sierra splashed water from the old-fashioned wash basin onto her face and neck, then straightened and used her worn flannel towel to dry herself. There was a water closet and bathroom down on the second floor, but Mr. Tellidine would be in it now. He was the house's earliest riser, since he worked for Thompson's Bakery delivering bread and pastries to the financial district's restaurants before they opened for business each day.

Waiting outside the bathroom door would be Mr.

Goshen, rubbing at his grizzled beard, muttering to himself. Sierra pitied him. He had been a speculator back in the '80's and had made a fortune in stocks, then lost it all. It had cost him part of his sanity. He sold buttons and notions for the T.C. Kellermant Company now, lugging his big black case aboard the train at least twice a week to call on his accounts in Napa and Sacramento. Twice a month he boarded the ferry and crossed over to Oakland to sell his goods to the dry-goods stores there. He always complained that in Oakland, the ranchers' wives were two years behind the fashion, and in San Francisco the women were two years ahead.

Mr. Goshen was harmless, but he mumbled almost constantly when no one was talking to him, mostly about the unfairness of life. Sierra could hardly argue with him on that score, but his bitterness scared her. Life had dealt her a bad hand as well, but she was determined not to slide into a sad and angry middle age. *She* was going to find a way out of the mission district.

Sierra giggled at herself. "It's so simple. I will marry a good man, work very hard with him at whatever his business is, and love him forever." She arched her back and stretched, yawning. Perhaps—she allowed herself to think it—she had already found the perfect man. "Mrs. Cameron Slade," she said aloud. Then she blushed.

Joseph Harlan was riding hard over the rocky ground. His horse was lathered with sweat, its breathing labored and ragged, but he kept his spurs against its sides.

3

∽

When the ranchhouse finally came into view, a lazy curl of smoke coming from the chimney, he scanned the outbuildings and corrals as he galloped closer. He needed his father—or better yet, Mr. Bigger—but he couldn't spot anyone but old Charley Fairs, mucking out the milk cow's stall.

Reining in beside the corral, Joseph hit the ground running and flung the door open wide. His father and Bigger were standing before the hearth, coffee cups cradled in their work-roughened hands.

"Bigger and I were just settling up what needs doing before we leave for the city in the morning," Joseph's father said. Then he narrowed his eyes. "What's wrong?"

"That Kentucky blood mare, Pa," Joseph began, then had to stop, as out of breath as if he had run the distance on foot.

"She foaling?" Bigger demanded, setting his coffee down and heading for the door before Joseph could get another word out.

"Yes," Joseph managed to answer as he followed Bigger, his father right behind him.

"Where?" Bigger shouted over his shoulder.

Joseph dragged in a long breath. "Up in Rocky Point meadow, and she's having trouble."

"Good thing you found her," Joseph's father said approvingly as they filed through the door, boots clattering across the porch. He took in Joseph's heaving horse and the corrals in one quick glance, then shouted in Charley's general direction, "Catch up my gray, then pull the tack off this one for Joseph's bay mare."

"I'll get my gelding," Bigger said, starting to run toward the bunkhouse corral.

Joseph sprinted after his father, the clean morning air cool against his face, the wild arch of the sky pale blue overhead.

Twirling around her little bedroom, Sierra put off getting ready for work for a few more precious minutes. She curtsied, humming a waltz she had heard the dining-room orchestra play. Maybe she would be going to balls and soirees at the Palace Hotel soon, instead of cleaning its rooms.

She flushed again. Cameron *had* asked her to come see him before work today. The invitation was highly improper, certainly, but he had been quick to assure her that she could remain in the hallway—that all he wanted to do was to talk to her about something important.

Sierra drew in a long shivery breath, then let it out in a whoosh as she rehung her towel on the washstand hook. "Today could be the day," she whispered. "Cameron might want to confess his attraction to me—maybe even his love." She closed her eyes, daring to hope.

Cameron always smiled the instant he saw her, and his dark eyes were always soft and attentive, as though every word she spoke was of grave import to him. It made Sierra giddy to think about his beautiful eyes, the fine shining brown of his hair, the breadth of his shoulders. He walked like a prince—like a man who owned every room he strode into. If he did love her, everything would change forever.

Sierra turned in a circle, pretending to waltz across a polished dance floor, barely managing her second turn before bumping into the bed and giggling again. "A fine, graceful wife I am going to make," she scolded herself.

Carefully pinching the thin muslin of her nightgown, she pretended to lift a heavy-hemmed velvet ball gown. Slowly, her head held high, she began to waltz again, more carefully, letting the dream take her for a moment. As Mrs. Cameron Slade, she wouldn't ever have to come back to this shabby little boardinghouse—except to get Mama's trunk. Inside it were a few clothes, her mother's silver hairbrush and her father's prayer book. Those were the only things in this dreary place that she cared anything about.

Sierra stopped dancing, suddenly ashamed of herself. She cared about Mrs. Evans. The old woman had been motherly in her curt, cantankerous way, and it meant a great deal to Sierra.

Sierra bit at her lower lip. Maybe Cameron would agree to take in Mrs. Evans. She was pleasant enough if people were respectful to her, and she was very strong in her way, even though she resembled a fragile wading bird with her thin legs and long neck. Sierra imagined dancing away into a golden sunset with the handsome and kind Mr. Slade, a lovely chamber in their large house set aside for Mrs. Evans.

Closing her eyes, Sierra made heaven a promise. If she got the chance, she would join the famous and generous Mrs. Hearst and her friends in charity committees. She would even join that odd, fiery Mother

Mary McDermott of the Flying Rollers of the House of David—and anyone else who was trying to help the poor orphans of San Francisco.

Sierra smiled, picturing herself sweeping down the sidewalk in a dress of fine silk, a smart hat, and spotless gloves. She would build an orphanage! It would be clean and sunny, and the children would never be whipped or frightened with stories of hellfire. They would be taught skills with which to support themselves their whole lives, and they would be allowed time to play: the very antithesis of St. Luke's Orphanage. They would be happy, not sad and terrified as she had been. How she had dreaded the coldly pious nuns! Only sisters with merry voices and love to give would be allowed to teach in her orphanage.

Sierra caught her breath and laughed aloud at the grandiosity of her fancies. "Silk dresses and philanthropy, indeed!" she whispered, staring at the battered trunk that held her whole inheritance.

Feeling breathless and silly and acutely aware of her threadbare nightgown, she parted the heavy bombazine curtains. She had made them from an old striped walking dress Mrs. Evans had given her. It had been designed way back in the '60's, Mrs. Evans had told her, during the War Between the States. The fashion then had been hooped skirts so wide two women could not pass each other on the sidewalks. There had been twenty yards and more of heavy bombazine in the old walking dress—more than enough for a pair of flounced curtains.

Sierra peeked out, then opened the curtains wide.

Behind the heavy cloth, the little square of a window was ebony black. Not a single amber twinkle from a neighbor's gas lamp, not a flicker of the electric lights in tall buildings up on Market Street. It was as though the world had disappeared. The fog was even thicker than usual this morning.

Impulsively, Sierra pulled up the sash and stood before the window in her nightgown. No one could see in this morning, that much was sure. She leaned out and looked down toward the street. The sound of delivery boys popping their buggy whips and a distant automobile motor came through the heavy mist. She could hear Mr. Hansen coughing in the room below hers. His asthmatic breathing was terrible sometimes, but he would eventually fall back to sleep, she knew. He wouldn't be getting up for hours. His work at the Harkenstein saloon didn't start until noon.

Shivering again as the mist began to float inside, Sierra closed the window and began to dress. She pulled off her nightgown and slid into her chemise and vest. Then she sat on her narrow hearth to unroll her thick woolen stockings, enjoying the faint warmth in the stone, a lingering gift from last night's tiny fire. There was a small gray ring of ashen clinkers. She had used only a little of her precious hoard of coal.

Mrs. Evans gave them a bargain. She sold lump and walnut coal to her tenants by the bucket for only a little more than she paid for it by the ton. It was soft and burned slow and smokey, but it was better than nothing. Wood was too dear for common folks. Only people up on Nob Hill had fireplaces with sweet-smelling logs crackling in them. The rest of the city put up with the oily stink of coal.

Sierra extended one leg, then the other, sliding her feet into her stockings. Then she stood to pull them up, still quivering with the chill. She wished that spring would hurry and arrive. How much longer could it be before the nights warmed up?

Sierra pulled on her stocking supporters next, straightening the elastic so it wouldn't cut into her skin. Janie at work kept talking about a new sort of stocking with unbleached cotton feet and soles. She swore they rested her feet, that now she never had to soak them in Epsom salts after work. Sierra's feet didn't hurt too much yet, but she knew by the time she was twenty-five or so they would. Poor Janie was forty-four, and the hard work at the Palace was almost more than she could manage now.

Sierra pulled her corset from the hook inside her wardrobe. The head housekeeper at the Palace was strict about tardies and the staff supervisor was even worse. Any girl who was late more than once or twice—with or without an excuse—stood in danger of losing her position. Sierra allowed herself one more quick daydream . . . a familiar one. She pictured herself telling Mrs. Halloran to tell the staff supervisor that she was quitting. Sierra changed this exhilarating last-day-at-work fantasy a little each time she permitted herself to have it at all.

At first she had imagined herself gray-haired, accepting a gold watch as a reward for long years of service to the hotel. Then, when she had first begun learning to sew, she had entertained the fancy that her hard and careful work had attracted the eye of some wealthy patroness who simply insisted on setting her up in her own shop. But this morning, Sierra imagined herself leaning close to Mrs. Halloran's unhappy visage to whisper the best excuse of all for her lateness—that Cameron Slade had proposed and had forbidden her to work another day.

Laughing, Sierra crossed her arms and reached around her waist to pull the corset laces tight, then brought the strings to the front to tie them. She glanced at her starched white uniform hanging on the tatty old dress form beside her washstand. The form was another gift from Mrs. Evans, a leftover from her days as a modiste, before her eyesight had failed and she couldn't sew.

For an instant Sierra squinted, letting her imagination turn the white linen cloth of her uniform into cascading chiffon and lace. She hadn't really told Cameron that she was an orphan yet. Would he be upset when he found out that he would be the one paying for the wedding?

Sighing guiltily, knowing that her mother wouldn't have approved for an instant of such time-wasting fancies, Sierra looked out her window again, not to daydream but to gauge the time. There was no glimmer of a distant sun to the east, no sparkle at all in the dense fog—but it was turning grayish now, so it was about 4:30.

As she combed and braided her dark hair, Sierra began to hum an old Irish melody. It had been one of

Mama's favorites, a quick-time tune for fiddlers. Mama might not have approved of her daydreams, but she would be looking down from heaven proud and pleased if they came true. So would her Da, Sierra was sure. She remembered them as perfect, loving, and wonderfully kind. But they had died when she was barely seven. Mrs. Evans said that if her parents had lived a few years longer, she would have begun to see them as people with flaws and faults. But they hadn't.

Sierra looked in her mirror and forced a smile. The orphanage had fed and clothed her until she was ten. Now she had a good position, a kind landlady, and a warm room. That was more than some could say. There was no point in having sad thoughts about her past—not on a day that promised to be the beginning of her bright and happy future. Sierra pinched her cheeks to heighten the pink flush that was always there. If Cameron didn't announce his intentions today, he might soon enough.

Riding eastward down the foggy road toward home, Daniel Gibbons knew he was in for a day or more of trouble with his wife. He had stayed up half the night walking Oakland's dim streets, and ended up at Jim Callister's saloon playing poker. He'd won some money at the poker table, but the winnings weren't enough to keep Sarah from lecturing him once again about the evils of drinking and gambling. His wife, the former Miss Sarah Mason, was a goody-goody from her head to her shoes.

Daniel was tired of Sarah's long-winded lectures. He had heard far too many of them in the three short years they had been married. Sarah was a temperance believer. She hated hard drink and everything that went with it—especially gambling and saloon girls. Loose women, she called them.

Daniel reined in his gelding, looking out over the bay at the fog bank that hid the distant city of San

Francisco. That was where he wanted to live—not here, where people's idea of a good time was a cattle auction or a horse sale. The ranch hands liked cards and drink, but they were dirty and smelled like their work.

Daniel's gelding arched its neck, trying to loosen the reins. The horse was hungry and tired and wanted to cover the muddy ground quickly. He didn't. Why hurry home to a lecture and an argument?

Fog-blurred figures in the distance caught Daniel's eye and he leaned forward, squinting. There were two riders approaching. No, it was three—two men and a woman riding sidesaddle. As they got closer he could see that all three had the practiced ease that came from hours in the saddle. "Ranchers," Daniel said aloud. "All dressed up to go to town."

Daniel watched the woman, who was riding a spirited, dancing horse. She kept well in front of the two men. She had the slim wasp waist of a girl, and the spill and drape of her chocolate brown riding skirt looked expensive even from afar. Daniel didn't need Sarah to whisper in his ear that her outfit fit a bit too close, even for fashion. He could appreciate that fact for himself as the young woman rode toward him.

As the distance between himself and the riders closed, Daniel stared at the stern fierce face of the older of the two men. He looked familiar . . . then Daniel recognized him. Ben Harlan. One of the smart big-money boys who had bought in at the right time and made a fortune in beef cattle. He was a fixture at election time, always campaigning for the railroaders' candidates. All the cattlemen wanted railheads every five miles. Why not? They made their money by shipping their cows to markets in the Midwest or even back East if the price was high enough.

Daniel focused his tired mind and opened his bloodshot eyes as the riders approached. It was well known that the Harlan girl wore clothing copied from the little dolls sent over from Paris, France, every spring. Sarah would want to know everything—the color of the fabric, the cut, her hat and gloves, the way her hair was dressed.

"Good morning," the young woman said as she passed Daniel. He tipped his hat, then touched it again to greet Ben Harlan. The young man who brought up the rear was unquestionably Harlan's son. He had his father's striking, angular face, but his eyes were soft blue, not his father's too-light icy blue. He touched his hat, and Daniel returned the gesture.

Once all three had passed, Daniel turned in his saddle to watch them ride into the fog again and out of sight. The girl's skirt had an odd and fancy pleating along the hem, her hat was topped with three nodding ostrich plumes. Weren't they out of style? Sarah would surely want to know all the details.

Daniel began to whistle as he let his gelding have its head. The lecture might not last more than half an hour or so. He would wait until Sarah ran down a little, then mention the Harlans casually, as if he wasn't sure they would interest her.

Salvation comes from odd places, Daniel thought, smiling. *This is the kind of mystery Sarah loves. Fancy that—*

*the well-known Harlans, out riding just past dawn dressed
for the opera, almost. On their way across the bay certainly.
The old man had looked angry, the son had looked worried
. . . Oh, yes, Sarah would want to know!*

"Joseph? Hold up."

Joseph Harlan ignored his sister's irritated glance
and reined in at the sound of their father's voice.
"Yes, Pa?"

"Call me Father."

"Father," Joseph echoed. He had to admit that the
more formal address fit this morning. He wasn't used
to seeing Pa dressed in gentleman's clothes. Usually,
when Pa left the ranch to go into San Francisco, he
traveled alone.

Pa spurred his gelding and caught up, reining in to
ride alongside Joseph. "Bigger says the foal is going to
live."

Joseph nodded.

"The mare, too, thanks to you. If you had missed
them, the coyotes would have gotten the foal, weak as
the dam was afterward."

"So Bigger told me." Joseph watched his father, sure
that the blood mare and her foal weren't the reason he
had ridden closer to talk. They had covered all this in
the barn outside the stall.

Abruptly, Camille gave her nervous mare more rein
and cantered farther out into the lead. She sat her
sidesaddle perfectly, shoulders back, head high, the
long silk of her riding skirt covering her boots.

"I'm worried about her," Ben Harlan muttered.

15

Joseph nodded. So was he. Camille was delightful and he loved her. She was also the kind of rebellious beauty who all too often came to no good.

"I'd marry her off in an instant if there was a suitor I thought deserved her."

Joseph turned to face his father, trying to ignore the unfamiliar clothing that made him look like a stranger. The black woolen trousers looked odd against saddle leather, and Pa's usual high-crowned hat had been traded for a stiff black bowler that sat high on his forehead. He looked more like a high-stakes gambler than a rancher.

"I want to settle you both in the next few years," Pa was saying.

Joseph nodded vaguely, hoping not to get his father started. By "settle," Pa meant married. Joseph was twenty-one and in no hurry. Pa seldom let him off the ranch, and there had been little opportunity to meet young women. The occasional dance out in Grass Valley was welcome entertainment, but he had known most of the girls all his life. Even the pretty ones seemed like sisters. They were all Camille's friends.

"May I gallop, Father?" Camille called, reining in and twisting around in her sidesaddle to face them. "Brandy wants a good run."

Pa grunted and nodded. "Watch her footing, it's . . . sand," Pa said, pausing because Camille was already gone, her hat-plumes flying as the mare rose into a canter, then flattened, stretching out into a hoof-pounding gallop.

Joseph watched his sister for a few seconds, then

turned toward his father again. "You'll never get her to marry someone you choose, Pa—Father," he added, correcting himself.

"She is as strong-willed as your mother was," Pa agreed.

"Not just strong-willed," Joseph said quietly, nudging the gelding into a jog. His father followed suit. Neither one of them was comfortable letting Camille simply thunder out of sight. Nor did they want to appear to be chasing her.

"I know," Pa said after a few seconds. "She's got a wild streak." He hitched himself up, standing in his stirrups to stretch. "And that's half the reason we're going into the city for a few months."

Joseph grinned at his father. "I thought you wanted me to meet the cattle buyers, and for both of us to see Caruso sing and go to a few dances, and. . . ."

"I do," his father cut him off. "But I also want to have you both about settled by the end of the stay. Camille of course—but you too, Joseph."

Joseph leaned down, pretending to straighten his stirrup. His father might want to see him engaged within a few months, but San Francisco seemed a foolish place to look for a ranch wife. The *Alta* and the *Examiner* were always full of gossip about each year's crop of society belles. He didn't want that kind of girl.

"I don't want to marry yet," he said aloud.

His father nodded. "But you will when you meet the right young lady."

Joseph shook his head. "How will I know her? By

the bounce of her hat feathers? The price of her dress? That's not love."

"You sound like Mr. Sharon this morning, Joseph, bitter about a love that turned cold."

"That scandal happened the year I was born, Pa," Joseph said, laughing.

"It did," his father agreed. "But you have heard of Sarah Althea Hill?"

Joseph nodded. "Of course, but—"

"That's what I want to spare you, son. And myself. We don't have a fortune to match Sharon's but we have enough to attract that kind of woman and that kind of nonsense. Althea ruined him, you know, then went insane herself. Affairs of the heart always end badly." Joseph watched his father reposition his stiff new hat. "Your mother and I were a good match. I respected her entirely."

Joseph kept his eyes on his sister in the distance. She had brought her mare back in hand and was cantering in a wide half-circle, probably setting up to gallop back to them. He didn't answer his father and the conversation died, as he had hoped it would.

Riding through the streets of Oakland, Joseph dropped back and let his sister's animated chatter entertain Pa. Camille was in high spirits, at least. She looked beautiful, her cheeks were flushed from the chilly air, her gloved hands sure and skilled upon the reins of her high-strung mare. Joseph looked across the street and saw two men turning to watch her pass. Pa was right to worry about her.

The road down to the ferry was muddy. The endless

spring fogs kept everything wet. When they dismounted at the livery stable Camille lifted her skirt well above her ankles, drawing a glare from Pa even though no one was close enough to see. She made a pouty face and walked the aisle between the stalls back to the road. Joseph followed Pa into the livery office.

"How long?" the man was asking.

"For my gelding, a few months, so I will need your boy to exercise him. I have a man riding in tonight to take the other two back to the ranch."

The man hooked his thumbs into his suspenders. "How about three months and a day's board charge now, and we can settle up on the rest later, Mr. Harlan?"

Joseph watched his father nod, then turned to flip the pages of a Sears, Roebuck catalogue lying on the liveryman's desk. He saw riding outfits not much different from Camille's that were priced at less than a quarter of what her dressmaker charged Pa. *Pa regards it as a good investment, though*, Joseph thought. *If Camille is going to interest a young man of good family and financial substance, she will be expected to look the part.*

Joseph flipped past the men's hats and stopped on a page with drawings of riding tack. He needed a new stock saddle for a gelding Pa had given him. The animal was so broad-backed there wasn't a saddle on the ranch that didn't pinch-fit it. Joseph let a few more pages fall and realized he was looking at women's corsets. He closed the catalogue, glancing up. Pa and the liveryman were talking horses now. Pa had seen a good mare in one of the stalls.

Joseph wandered out the door, his boots making a

hollow rhythm on the planked sidewalk. He stood in the fog-chilled air, looking up at the sky. It had been a clear dawn, promising a sunny day at home. They had ridden into the fog bank that blanketed the coast every morning. He looked down the street. Camille had walked half a block.

"Joseph!" she called when she saw him. "I hear the foghorn. Make Papa hurry!"

Joseph shouted back to Pa and got a terse response. Camille put on her pouty face again, her gloved hands on her hips. She was standing on a board laid across the mud in front of the livery, her skirts safe from the morass. Her tight-laced waist was slim as a little girl's, her back bent into a fashionable "S" shape by the steel in her corset. She looked like an illustration from Godey's, with her hair tucked beneath her hat, a loosened tendril or two falling down the nape of her neck. Up the street, men stood in front of a blacksmith's shop looking at her. Joseph glared at them until they turned away.

"Father?" Joseph shouted, turning back in to the livery, emphasizing the formal address Pa had been trying to drill into them. Then he looked back at his sister. She was flicking her forefinger at her shoulder. No doubt a spatter of mud from Brandy's dancing hooves had soiled the cloth.

Joseph grinned. The trunks—all of them already freighted to the Palace Hotel—contained a number of gowns, all flattering and fashionable, all expensive. In fact, Camille's wardrobe made up nearly three quarters of what they had packed for this journey to the city. Pa had borne the wagon-loading grimly and silently.

"Let's get down to the landing," Pa said, emerging from the office. His tone was brisk, as though he needed to urge them along. Joseph turned to hide his grin and fell into step just behind his father.

As they caught up with her, Camille lifted her skirts again, dancing along the board. With an agile little jump at the end, she leapt the last of the puddles and landed on the cobblestones. She smiled winningly over her shoulder, and Pa offered her his arm—as if she suddenly needed help navigating a little mud.

Joseph followed them, walking a little apart, frowning now. He wasn't going to let Pa railroad him into a marriage he didn't want. As much as he loved his sister, he didn't want anything to do with the kind of girls she was trying to emulate.

Mama had been a real partner to his father. Though she had been small-boned and pretty, she had still ridden the fences and helped with branding and stayed up all night at calving time. Joseph knew that his father had been a little ashamed of her, with her striding walk and her unfrilled dresses and sunpinkened face. But she had been exactly the kind of woman Joseph wanted to marry one day. He didn't want a glass-house orchid. He wanted a field poppy.

"I don't think I'll find the kind of woman who will charm me at the Palace," he said quietly, not intending his father to hear—but hear he did, and he answered— with a single, clipped word.

"Nonsense."

3

Mrs. Evans stopped to catch her breath, gripping the feather duster. Going up to the third floor was getting to be a chore. Her bones ached. This weather was enough to make a cripple out of anyone old enough to have lost a son and a husband in the War Between the States.

Glancing back down the stairs, she leaned on the banister. This old boardinghouse was getting to be more than she could handle, and she knew it. She grimaced. The boarders were her only income.

"Should have gotten married again," she said to herself, as she started upward again, heavy-footed and slow. "Should have taken up with that fool James Barnett, like Daddy wanted me to do."

She clumped another step, then another, still talking to herself. "He was a miserable tyrant of a man, though. Livinia Roark found that out soon enough after she married the old—"

"Good morning, Mrs. Evans!"

The bright, young voice startled Mrs. Evans, and she gripped the railing, glaring up the stairs at Sierra. The girl was always so damnably cheerful. "Good morning, Sierra," she said aloud.

The girl looked pretty this morning, as usual. Her dark hair was wound into a halo of braids, shining and clean. "I apologize if I startled you, Mrs. Evans," she was saying.

Mrs. Evans nodded, pausing again. Her right knee was throbbing in time with her heart. It was swollen again, who knew why? Gout didn't start in the knees, she was pretty sure.

"Is everything all right?" Sierra asked. Her peaches-and-cream skin was even prettier when it was chilly.

Mrs. Evans sighed, gripping the handrail to take part of her weight off of her knee. "I was coming up to see to the dusting."

Sierra was looking into her eyes as if trying to divine her thoughts—it was most discomfiting, this direct stare the girl had. But she was unfailingly kind and honest—and helpful. The house was brighter and better since she had moved in two years before.

"If it will wait until I get home today," Sierra said smiling warmly, "I'll be happy to do it then."

Mrs. Evans nodded. "That would be a help." She watched Sierra patter past, going down the stairs like a ten-year-old boy, jumping down the last two at the landing. If the girl didn't marry well enough, or didn't marry at all, perhaps they would be able to work out an arrangement so that Sierra could manage the place in trade for her rent and board.

Mrs. Evans listened to the thumping footsteps as Sierra ran across the parlor. She was very pretty, but she was like a colt, not a young lady. Perhaps the men with real prospects would pass her by, seeing her lack of refinement. The kind of poverty Sierra came from left coarse scars that no man of wealth wanted in a wife. If she married a brick mason or a hotel bellman, or some such fellow, he would see the advantage in paying no rent, Mrs. Evans was sure. It could all work out to everyone's advantage.

The front door opened, the bell on the knob jangling as Sierra hurried out. Something had the girl excited this morning, Mrs. Evans was sure. She was usually cheerful, but this skip-hop exuberance was different. Maybe she had already met the brick mason she would wed and was meeting him on the corner. Mrs. Evans turned slowly on the stairs and started downward, leaning hard on the handrail.

Sierra shivered as she turned up Decatur Street. It was short—barely a block long. Sierra got to the corner quickly, walking fast through the swirling fog. The cool wet air stung her cheeks. She ducked her head without slowing down.

Saloons and boardinghouses lined Bryant Street, interspersed with groceries and watchmakers and stationers. Most of the businesses were small, and had rooms to let above the shops. Nothing was open yet and the saloon swampers were leaving to go home, their night's mopping and cleaning finished; Sierra could see the gaslights inside still burning, for the bartenders and grill cooks who would soon be there to serve the earliest of the day's customers.

As she neared Sixth Street, Sierra heard voices behind her. She was never alone on the sidewalks at this hour. There were bakery boys and newspaper boys, and women who cleaned houses up on Nob Hill. There were reporters sometimes, too, the younger ones living in the boardinghouses down here on their slim salaries. Some of them were handsome, and a few had talked to Sierra on her way to work.

A man on the streetcar had asked her to dinner a few weeks before. But he had frightened her with his intense talk about the railroads buying votes, about how the money-men ran the city—and about how they should all be taken down a peg or two. His world seemed dangerous and angry, and Sierra had not wanted to spend any more time around him. So she had politely refused.

Danger and anger were too familiar. Two long years she had roamed the docks after she'd turned ten and had to leave St. Luke's, scrabbling for food with other forgotten children. It had seemed an eternity before she'd met old Paddy and been transported to the safe haven of Ingleside racetrack's quiet stables.

Saint Mary's bells began to toll in the distance, muted like every other sound this morning. Then the clock chimed again, snapping Sierra out of her thoughts. It was five o'clock. She *was* a little behind her usual schedule. "Too much daydreaming," she chided herself aloud, and lengthened her step.

Turning left onto Sixth Street, Sierra's shoe heel

skidded on the wet sidewalk, but she managed to catch her balance. Turning sideways to raise her skirt in order to step off the high curb, she heard voices again. This time she saw a shadowy group of men materialize out of the fog. They passed her tipping their hats, then disappeared into the mist again halfway across the street. They were all carrying thick black cases with straps and big nickel-plate buckles fastened tightly. The scent of their toilet water lingered in the cool air behind them.

Sales agents, Sierra was sure. The cases held samples of who-knew-what? Maybe fountain and stylographic pens and ink pots, or stereopticons with three-dimensional views of Paris and Niagara Falls—or perfumes or health elixirs or suspenders. The men would make their rounds, stopping at the dry goods and stationers stores—maybe even The Emporium or The White House or some other big department stores up around Union Square.

Another block up Sixth Street, Sierra had to half-turn and step off the curb again. The wire ribs of her corset dug into the small of her back as she crossed Harrison. She let her skirt fall back to cover her ankles and sighed. It wasn't a real corset—not the kind that gave a woman the incredibly graceful arched back that magazines called the Grecian Bend. But she couldn't afford a corset like that—and even if she had been able to, she couldn't have worn it to work. How would she have made a bed or scrubbed a floor?

Mrs. Evans thought all corsets were terrible for a woman's body, and everything she said made sense.

Sierra and every other woman she knew treasured the moment at night when she could undo the laces and unfasten the hooks and eyes and take her corset off. But still . . . Sierra quickened her pace again, sighing. So many of the women who stayed at the Palace were beautiful, like rare roses with slender stems.

A delivery wagon passed, the horses' shoes striking like muffled bells on the cobbles. Sierra smelled the warm odor of fresh bread pouring from an open door. The city was waking up now, the sidewalks were filling. Sierra heard people's voices now and then in the fog. It was not clearing. If anything it was getting even thicker.

Sierra was glad she always braided her hair and pinned it up. This fog would have made it positively a sight if she hadn't. Cameron had said he liked it like this, even though it was an old-fashioned style her mother had worn long ago. Sierra smiled. Cameron made her feel beautiful—and he *did* act like he cared for her.

Sierra longed to be able to really talk to him. She had to be so careful whenever she saw him, making sure that if Mrs. Halloran came down the hall she could instantly appear to be getting something from her cart and just answering a guest's casual remark in the course of her work.

"Excuse me, Miss," a man said behind her, and she caught her breath, startled when he materialized out of the fog. Then she felt foolish. A lot of people lived south of The Slot and worked up along Market Street, or somewhere farther. Sierra knew the crowds were thickening, as people came up the side streets and joined the parade headed toward Market Street and the streetcar lines—she just couldn't see them this morning. In another hour it'd be hard to get a seat. People would be hanging onto the straps and leaning outward, as the red cars rolled toward the financial district or Nob Hill.

Passing the Italian groceries on the corner of Howard and Sixth, Sierra could smell the sharp scent of fresh onions and basil, even though it would be another hour before the bins of vegetables were out under the awnings.

Sierra heard the clattering roar of an automobile as she stepped off the high curb. She paused long enough to make sure the sound was fading—that the vehicle was moving away from her—then hurried across the street. Two Chinese men passed her, almost running with the peculiar, gliding stride that always amazed Sierra. They were talking to each other, and seemed not to notice her at all.

There were shouts off to Sierra's left as she got back onto the sidewalk, then a slamming crash and the whinny of a frightened horse. More shouts followed. Glancing back, Sierra hoped the poor horse hadn't been hurt—or either of the drivers. Horses got so frightened by the automobiles, and there were more and more of them in the city now. Rich men's toys, Cameron said. He didn't believe the autos would be around in ten years except in museums. Sierra disagreed—but she hadn't said so.

Cameron had very strong opinions, and the last

thing Sierra wanted to do was to upset him. If the autos were still in use ten years hence, she would remind him that he had so vehemently predicted the opposite, and they would have a little laugh together.

"Mrs. Cameron Slade," Sierra whispered to herself, then covered her mouth with her hand. It was probably bad luck to say it aloud. Mama had always warned against bad luck. Da had not believed in anything but hard work and God. Sierra's eyes flooded and she blinked back the tears. Even after twelve years, even though sometimes she felt like she couldn't remember their faces anymore, she missed her parents terribly.

The streetcar bell was already ringing as Sierra rounded the corner. She picked up her skirt to run, taking careful, short steps to avoid slipping on the sidewalk. As she hesitated on the edge of the sidewalk, a man came out of the mist to her right and offered his arm. She murmured her thanks and let him steady her as she crossed the cobblestones. The streetcar was braking to a halt, the bell ringing madly now.

"Thank you so much," Sierra said breathlessly as the man courteously helped her into the car. He released her elbow, smiled, then directed his attention elsewhere, relieving her of the need to make polite conversation. She was grateful. Talking to strangers was often hard for her. She usually ended up feeling awkward and sounding silly. Sierra presented her transfer ticket for punching, then turned to find a seat as the conductor waved her toward the rear of the car.

"A pretty girl like you should have an escort," a dapper-looking man in the first row of seats said as she walked past. Sierra pretended not to hear him. Men often said something like that to her. But what was she supposed to do? Her parents were no longer living, and she had no brothers and no beau.

Livvy and Jane, two of the girls Sierra worked with, had shuddered when she told them that she lived alone. Her landlady didn't like it either. But Mrs. Evans was a long-time widow, so at least she understood that some things were forced on a person, not chosen. She had lost her son and her husband in the War, long before Sierra had been born, and she had lived alone ever since—except for her boarders, of course.

Sierra slipped into a seat halfway back and smoothed her skirt. The man who had helped her cross the street went past, nodding politely once more. He looked about forty, Sierra thought. Old enough to be her father. And he had a very kind face. She watched him seat himself toward the rear of the car, arranging his gloves and cane, then resetting his hat as the streetcar lurched back into motion.

Sierra tried to imagine her own father's face. He had never had soft leather gloves—or a cane, for that matter. He had been a mason. He had laid brick all his life, proud of the calluses on his hands and the mortar sand under his nails.

Sierra watched the Spreckles Building glide past, then the Parrot Building. Both looked enormously dark and dreary, their stone stained with the fog's chill and wet. The Academy of Sciences looked just as bleak as it appeared out of the fog, short and squat next to the enormous Flood Building looming beside it. The car stopped and passengers came down the aisle.

"May I?"

"Of course." Sierra gathered up her skirt once more as a gentleman sat beside her. His suit was respectable, if a little shabby. He pulled off his hat and wiped his sleeve across his domed forehead, then replaced the hat. Then he stared ahead as the car started up again in little lurches. Sierra kept her eyes straight ahead. No one was talking much this morning. Everyone seemed distant, insulated by the fog. Even the conductor's shouts and the ringing of the silver bell seemed dulled.

Sierra ducked to look out from under the canopy as they passed the Phelan Building across the street. So many of the buildings were named after the men who had built them. Would there ever be a Slade Building? Sierra blushed as the car stopped, brakes grinding, at the corner of Market and Fourth. When it jigged back into motion, the shabby man was gone and an older woman had taken his place. Her clothes were beautifully hand sewn. The fabric of her dress was Moire silk, with water patterns that made it almost iridescent.

"Whatever are you staring at, Miss?" she said sharply.

"I apologize," Sierra responded instantly, startled and embarrassed by the woman's irritation, swallowing the compliment that had been on the tip of her tongue. She blushed again and looked straight forward. The Call Building was on the right now, its upper stories disappearing into the fog.

"I'm a modiste," the woman said brusquely as the car stopped and Sierra stood up to get out. "If your mistress needs a dressmaker, you may tell her Mildred Attony of Van Ness and Fulton Streets is available to design and sew for women of quality."

Sierra mumbled something polite and made her way down the aisle between the seats. Her feet were cold. The car steps were slick with condensed fog. As she stepped down onto the cobblestones, a surrey passed just behind her going the other way. The horses' hooves made a hollow clopping sound as the driver whipped them up. It was a fine team, Sierra saw, long-legged with finely sprung ribs and deep chests—almost blooded enough for the racetrack.

The horses shook their manes and lashed their fog-sodden tails, their ears flattened against their heads. The driver was pushing them dangerously fast and they seemed to resent it. Sierra watched, disapproving. If a child or an old person crossed at the wrong moment in this thick fog, something awful could happen.

The streetcar bell rang its high silvery note again and rolled forward as Sierra walked across the street, glancing both ways. Stepping back up onto the sidewalk, she saw misty figures walking in and out of the grand double-doored Market Street entrance of the Palace. There were shops all along the ground floor on this side, but none of them were open yet. Sierra was about to turn toward Third Street—housekeepers were only allowed to enter from the Mission Street entrance—when a familiar silhouette caught her eye, and she paused. Cameron.

From where she stood, it was impossible for Sierra to see the gold-brown of his curly hair or the little scar that marred his left cheek, but she could imagine every detail of his face perfectly. She had longed to ask him about the scar. Maybe it was from some boyhood exploit gone wrong. Or maybe it was something far more exciting than that. He had been to Europe, she knew that much. He had told her a little about his travels in France and Italy.

Cameron turned, facing away from her, his outline muted and unsharp, like a watercolor painting. Invisible in the fog, an automobile roared past, the clattering din lasting longer than usual. The driver was no doubt driving cautiously this morning. Sierra stood still. Cameron was pulling out his watch, checking the time. Abruptly, he started off in the opposite direction. In just a few strides, the fog came between them and he disappeared.

He has forgotten, then, Sierra thought, her eyes stinging. Or perhaps some very important business had come up and there had been no time to wait and tell her. She felt her sense of expectation seep away. In its place was the clammy cold of the fog that filled the street. She began to walk very slowly toward the side entrance, blinking back tears.

Mrs. Halloran put her hands on her hips. Her back hurt. She had slept badly again, tossing and turning and wishing she had a little laudanum left. She was going to have to start keeping it on hand.

She glanced down the hall. It was almost six o'clock.

Twenty-four of her twenty-five girls were here and already tying on their aprons and arranging stacks of linen on their pushcarts. Mrs. Halloran caught Miss De Loran's eye and tapped her temple. De Loran reached up to tuck the stray wisp of hair back into place.

Mrs. Halloran checked the clock on the wall, then looked down the long hall with its spotless linoleum floor. The overhead electric bulbs were painfully bright. She blinked. "Damn that girl! Where is Miss O'Neille?"

"Mrs. Halloran," a soft, musical voice said from behind her. "I think that Sierra told me to tell you that she might be a little late this morning."

Mrs. Halloran gave up staring down the hallway and turned stiffly to face the pale girl with her over-large teeth. "What, Miss Hale?"

"I said I think that Sierra told me she'd be late today."

Mrs. Halloran stiffened, amazed afresh at how foolish these girls nowadays were. This one was always talking about other people's troubles in her soft, tentative voice. Perhaps she had no troubles of her own to keep her busy yet. Mrs. Halloran shook her head. "Livvy, why would I believe that? Wouldn't Sierra have told me herself?"

Livvy had the good grace to blush. "I . . . I wouldn't know that, Ma'am. But she said that—"

"Horsefeathers," Mrs. Halloran muttered. "Miss Hale, you are a terrible liar. And it is not a skill a young lady should *try* to acquire, do you think?"

Livvy was bright red now. The rose patches on her

cheeks looked hot enough to burn. The clock began to strike and Mrs. Halloran turned to look down the hallway again.

On the third strike, the lift doors at the end of the corridor opened and Miss O'Neille tumbled out, coming down the hall at a half-run, skirts flying, eyes red as though she had been weeping.

"Slow down!" Mrs. Halloran called to her and the awkward girl stumbled to a fast walk, patting at that mass of silly old-fashioned braids she seemed to favor. "Get your cap on," Mrs. Halloran said sternly.

Miss O'Neille actually squeaked as she realized what she had forgotten. She thrust her hands in her coat pockets to fish out her white maid's cap. Settling it on her hair, she slowed, then stopped. "I am so sorry that I'm late," she began.

"Oh, but you weren't," Miss Hale spoke up, interrupting her. "Not quite. I mean the clock was still striking and—"

"Miss Hale—" Mrs. Halloran scolded.

"It's all right Livvy," Miss O'Neille said swiftly. "I was almost late and—"

"But only almost!" Miss Hale whispered. "You made it before the third strike and—"

"Enough, girls!" Mrs. Halloran interrupted, unable to listen to another silly word. She pressed her hands against the small of her back. "Get your lists."

"I suppose we have enough to do beyond scolding nice girls?" someone asked.

Mrs. Halloran scanned the faces, trying to decide who had spoken. She really wanted someone to blame for the insolence, and she was almost sure it had been Celia Gonzales, one of the older women. But all the faces—thin, full, young, middle-aged, plain, and pretty—were bland, opaque. Every single housekeeper in the line was seemingly absorbed in some tiny task like flicking lint from her uniform or straightening her cap. The older women stared at the floor, or the far wall, patient and silent. Celia looked at her fingernails, then half turned so that her expression was hidden.

Mrs. Halloran cleared her throat. "Front desk says we have a few over three hundred fifty checkouts."

Everyone made a little sighing sound and Mrs. Halloran glared at them. It was ridiculous. Did they expect to get paid without working for their money? The young people of the country were falling apart, getting soft and lazy and worse.

Mrs. Halloran stood at her post against the wall as the housekeepers shuffled through their preparation, checking their carts for rags, lemon-oil polish, lye soap, and ammonia. Miss O'Neille went down the hall to a storeroom and came back carrying a box of the cakes of perfumed soap that were left in every bathroom every day. She filled her basket, then handed the box on up the line.

"Are we ready?" Miss Halloran said, just loudly enough to startle the girls. There was a shuffling of feet, but no one spoke.

"The second shift will take most of the stock and service numbers today. We get the cleanouts." This time there was a murmur that ended when she frowned. She pressed at the small of her back again, waiting for one of them to be unwise enough to complain out loud. But there was no sound at all. It was as though they were all holding their breath.

She pulled down her note board and began handing out her lists, ticking off each girl's name as the carts wheeled past. She heard the washing machines start up in the big room down the hall. The kitchens would be coming to life one floor up. The hotel was waking up. Mrs. Halloran lifted her shoulders and rounded her back, trying to ease the pain.

4

Camille stepped off the ferry and waited for her father and brother to catch up, before crossing to the line of hacks waiting along the curb in front of the clock tower. She was positively glowing with excitement. "This is going to be so much more exciting than living on the ranch," she whispered into the fog. Then she glanced back. Papa and Joseph had their heads together again; they were talking money, she was sure of it. Money and cows were all they ever talked about. Or politics, but that usually ended in a shouting match, which Papa always won.

Camille swirled her skirts, holding them just a few inches above the graveled drive. She shrugged her shoulders, settling the band of steel that ran down her spine into a more comfortable position. She stood with her hips tipped forward—it was the only way the band of metal in her corset would allow her to stand.

"May I help you, Miss?" one of the drivers called.

She could tell by his grin that he found her pretty, and she smiled at him—a quick, innocent smile that Papa wouldn't see or be able to criticize even if he did.

"My father and brother are a bit slow this morning," Camille called back to the driver.

"Camille?" Papa said sternly from behind her. "Behave yourself."

"Yes, Papa," she said, remembering too late about the intimacy and privacy needed for addressing one's father as "Papa." It was absolutely inappropriate in public.

Camille held her tongue while her father chose another hack—one with a sullen, polite driver who opened the door without looking directly at any of them. Without so much as a trace of a smile, he offered his arm and helped her climb up, leaning away so that no part of her skirt so much as brushed the toes of his well-blacked boots.

Camille stepped up into the carriage and bent to sit carefully on the edge of the upholstered seat. It looked like an automobile seat, she noticed—all the rage the past few years. This driver's company had put serious money into making their hacks modern and fashionable. The driver closed the door.

Papa and Joseph were back to their cow talk, Camille noted as she settled her skirt and looked out the hack window. There was nothing to see, just acres and miles and eternities of fog—but she knew what was out there.

The whole wide, wonderful city of San Francisco was just waiting. There would be parties and dances and plays and entertainments. Camille glanced at her brother, and he smiled back at her. She flashed him an answering grin, which earned her a frown from their father, and she ducked her head, hiding her face until she could present a demure visage once again. She felt the carriage rock as the driver climbed up to his high seat. Papa leaned out the window and called out just two words to the driver.

"The Palace!"

"Yessir!" the driver responded, and the whip cracked in three sharp little pops over the horses' backs. The wheels turned as the team started off, steel tire rims grinding on the gravel as the driver guided the horses up out of the Embarcadero lot and onto the wide cobbled surface of Market Street. Out on the bay a foghorn sounded, a sad, lonely sound that made Camille shiver.

"Are you chilled?" Papa asked, and she realized that he had been watching her even while he spoke to Joseph.

She shook her head. "Just excited."

He smiled at her and she found herself beaming at him again, a smile too wide and too freely given to be ladylike. She tried to contain herself, but the truth was she was too keyed up. She could barely wait to get her first invitation to a ballroom dance. Surely someone they met would include her on a guest list? She was so afraid that no one would. She knew she wasn't bad-looking, and if she was careful to remember every-thing she had been taught by her tutors, she could behave like a proper lady, too—part of the hoi polloi, as Papa would say. All she wanted was for someone to give her a chance.

On the sidewalks a steady parade of people walked silently, none of them talking or laughing. Camille watched them as they appeared out of the fog, then disappeared again as the hack passed on. Most of them were wearing work clothes of one kind or another. The flocks of bankers and brokers in their black suits and two-inch collars and careful, muted ties would not be out until later.

Camille watched the grand facades of the buildings in the financial district slide past. This was the only part of the city that she knew at all. Coming to town with Papa had always meant visits to two different banks, a stop-in at the Olympic Club, and a quick run up to Union Square to shop for a dress or to the Emporium with its elevators and genteel, quiet-voiced clerks.

Camille refolded her hands and lifted her chin, trying to still her nervous excitement. Her corset was laced so tightly she would begin to feel faint or ill if she wasn't careful. For a full minute, she forced herself to simply look out the window, but her excitement kept nudging at her thoughts until she finally let it burst back through, helpless to contain it.

Three times since her fifteenth birthday—once each year—her father had taken her and Joseph to the Palace Grill for supper. Every time, Camille had watched the other guests, fascinated. The women amazed her. Their hats were magnificent. Their hair was always dressed in the latest fashions. The rustle of their gowns had made her feel like a child transported to a fairyland of silk and perfume. The men had frightened her a little with their imperious jocularity, the seeming certainty that whatever they asked for they would get—without ever having to so much as raise their voices. The first time it had taken her half the ride home to realize that the food had been absolutely delicious, too.

Suddenly, the great walls studded with brass disks came into sight. Camille tilted her head to look upward. The first two tiers of bay windows were visible—they were the trademark of the Palace—every room had a wonderful view of the city. She glanced at her father, and wondered how long he and Joseph had been sitting silently. They looked tense. Camille folded her hands in her lap.

"Our trunks should already be in the rooms," Papa said, touching her elbow and gesturing upward. She nodded.

"Let's get on with it, then," Joseph said. There was a decided tenseness in his voice.

Papa straightened. "Don't rush your sister. She is excited about all this."

Joseph nodded curtly and stepped down, as the driver opened the carriage door. Papa went next, offering his arm so that Camille could descend. She lifted her skirt and looked down to make sure she stepped squarely onto the carriage steps. Head high, mincing so that her skirts swayed, Camille let her father help her up onto the high curb. The ornate gas lamps on the sidewalk were still burning, making a triad of rose-amber globes of light in the mist.

As her father and brother stood side by side waiting for the driver, Camille took a single step into the fog. It was so thick, so like goose down this morning. Without warning, a young man appeared out of the dense mist and Camille took a quick step backward and stumbled. Snake-quick, his hand shot out and grabbed her arm before she could fall.

"I am so very sorry," he said in a polite voice.

Camille looked up into his handsome face, and when he smiled, she found herself smiling back at him.

"You just appeared, sir!"

His smile broadened. "You are the apparition, not I. And a lovely one, at that."

Camille felt herself blush as he bowed, stepped back and tipped his hat, then strode past, nodding politely. He touched his hat once more as he walked by Papa and Joseph. Then he was gone. Breathless, Camille turned to see another hack slant into the curb. The driver had barely stopped when two men got out talking in rapid-fire French. Camille could only try to look serene as they walked by her, completely absorbed in their discussion.

"Camille? Are you ready to go in?" Papa asked.

She spun around to face him. "Oh, yes!"

He laughed, then turned to Joseph. "One of us is excited, at least. Shall we?"

Camille made a face at Joseph as they passed him, and he made one back. Then, perfectly genteel, she accompanied her father and brother into the grand lobby of the Palace Hotel. It was as wonderful as she had remembered it. She swept across the thick carpeting, glancing up at the crystal chandeliers hanging from the high, ornate ceiling.

Joseph followed his sister and father through the maze of potted palms to the concierge's counter, then on to the elevator. The doors closed soundlessly; then there was a faint hissing noise, as the operator pulled the lever and the cage rose smoothly upward.

When the doors opened, the operator stepped out and looked down the hall. "Fourth floor, sir. And there is a porter here to assist you."

Joseph stepped out just behind Camille. A uniformed porter was hurrying toward them.

"Do you have luggage, sir?" he asked as he got closer.

Joseph stepped back and let his father explain that their trunks should already be in room 445. The porter half-bowed and graciously extended one arm, indicating that they should go before him. Camille took Pa's arm, a silly smile fixed on her mouth. Joseph wondered if it would leave her face the entire time they were here.

"And here we are, sirs and miss, here we are . . ." The porter took the key from Pa and Joseph watched him open the door, pushing it back to reveal the room. Joseph could see their belongings stacked against one wall, but the pile looked too small. Then he realized that the two biggest trunks were missing: Camille's clothes.

"My daughter's room adjoins this one?" Pa said, his voice rising enough to make it a question.

"That would be 446. Yes, sir."

Joseph watched the porter half-bow again, a practiced little motion.

"You two get settled," Pa said as the porter left. "I'm going to go down and talk to the front desk about staying another month."

"We just got here, Pa," Joseph said, astounded.

"Joseph, I am simply going to make the reservation. We can change our minds if need be. Is that all right with you?"

Joseph stared at his father. Pa was angry. Really angry. At what? As he watched his father stalk back down the hall, Joseph shook his head.

"Come on," Camille said, pulling at his arm. He let her lead him into the room. She shut the door behind them.

The room was big, Joseph saw—or at least it wasn't small. There were two beds, a low couch with dark wood and pearl gray upholstery, and wardrobes along the back wall. The window was big. He could see the milky outlines of the buildings across the street. The fog was thinning a little.

"Oh, look!" Camille squealed, sounding like a little girl who'd found a piece of cake in the cupboard. Joseph smiled. It was hard to resist her high spirits.

She was pulling him into the bathroom. "Look, Joseph look!"

He stared at the bathtub. It was bigger than any he had ever seen. And the faucet handles were as shiny as silver.

"It's long enough to stretch out in," Camille whispered.

Joseph nodded, smiling. It was.

"And look at the mirrors!"

Joseph turned to follow her gesture. The mirrors were long enough to show him a full-length view of his pretty sister, and, behind her, himself. He looked dour and unhappy, like a man worried about something grave.

"Does my room have one like this?" Camille asked, staring at him.

Joseph shook his head, helpless in the face of her breathless questioning. "How would I know, Camille?"

"Let's go *look*, Joseph!" She took his hand and pulled him to the adjoining door. It was unlocked, and she pushed it wide open. Unable to pull him along fast enough, she released his hand and ran through her bedchamber in ten quick strides. Her giggles told him that her bath was as deep and long as the one in the first bathroom.

"Oh, Joseph, isn't it wonderful?" she demanded, coming back out into the bedchamber.

"It is splendid," Joseph agreed. He glanced out the window again. There was a faint knocking sound from the room on the other side of theirs. It was barely audible, but it reminded him that each of the many doors on this hall had people behind it. The idea made him feel odd. He was going to be living in a building that held more people on a single floor than every home, cabin, bunkhouse and shack on their ranch.

"I am going to take a bath," Camille said from behind him. She nudged him back through the adjoining door. "Stay out for an hour or two. Tell Papa."

Joseph nodded absently at her. He was trying to work it out. There were probably six or seven hundred rooms. Maybe more like eight. If there were just two people in each of them. . . .

A knock on the door interrupted his thoughts. He went to open it, expecting to see his father or the porter. He fumbled with the lock release. A feminine voice said something from out in the hallway, but he couldn't understand the words through the heavy wooden door.

"Just a moment," he said loudly.

"Yes, sir," came the faint response.

Joseph finally managed to open the door, pulling it toward himself slowly. He saw a starched white uniform and the edge of an apron, and understood instantly what the woman had been trying to ask him.

"We've just now arrived," he began, "so we really don't need anything at. . . ."

He trailed off, unable to continue for an instant. The girl on the other side of the door was so pretty that her gray eyes and full mouth left him momentarily without words.

"Joseph?" It was Papa, standing awkwardly on the other side of the girl's pushcart. He tapped at the linens impatiently. "Miss, could you please move this contraption?"

"Oh yes, sir," she said apologetically, glancing once at Joseph, then at the cart as she pulled it out of Papa's way.

"Thank you, Miss," Joseph said, hoping that she would look up, that he would get to see her deep gray eyes again, but she didn't. She turned and pulled the cart down the hallway, looking down at a list of room numbers as she went. Her dark hair was pinned up in a mass of intertwining braids. He could see wisps of it working loose at the nape of her neck.

"Well, I made the reservations," Papa was saying, and Joseph turned to face him.

"Don't worry, Joseph," Pa said. "You'll get used to city life and then you won't want to go back out to the ranch. I'll make a businessman out of you yet!"

Joseph nodded vaguely, then stepped out into the hallway, pretending to look at the painting hung on the opposite wall. The girl's cart was only a few doors down, but he couldn't see her now.

5

The next morning, Sierra was walking back down the second floor hall from the linen closet when Cameron came out of his room. She was surprised. He was rarely up this early. Often she had to wait until after ten to make up his bed. He smiled, as he always did when he saw her.

"Good morning," he called out. She answered him and his smile broadened. "And how are you today?" he called cheerfully as he walked toward her.

Sierra blushed. He obviously didn't remember asking her to come talk to him before work the day before. And if Mrs. Halloran caught her talking to him in the hall, it could cost her her job.

Sierra slowed her step, but he strode straight toward her, not stopping until he was close enough to look into her eyes, his handsome face serious and intent. Her heart leapt.

"I wanted to ask you where you live," he said.

Sierra blinked, startled by the question—but if he noticed her reaction he ignored it.

"I have a cousin coming into town from Baltimore," he told her, then dropped his voice confidingly. "That whole side of the family is too proud to take any help from me. But I thought if I could find her a reasonable, decent place. . . ."

"Well it isn't fancy or—"

"She will be working as a clerk. Her father passed away when she was young and. . . ." He trailed off, his deep eyes sad.

Sierra recited the address, and watched as he pulled a small leather-bound book from his pocket and flipped through it to find a blank page. He wrote the address with deft, quick jabs of his pencil, then looked up.

"Thank you so much, Sierra." His voice was warm and his eyes lingered on hers. Sierra held the clean towels she was carrying to her chest and waited for him to say more. But he didn't. Instead he winked at her and grinned, then stepped around her, whistling as he started down the hall toward the elevators.

Sierra watched him go, then tried to push her hurt feelings aside as she walked on down the long hall. He meant nothing by it, she told herself over and over. He was a businessman, preoccupied with his own affairs. He was fond of her—she hadn't imagined that—but she had apparently overestimated the depth of his feeling . . . If she waited, his feelings might grow.

She stacked the towels on her cart, still thinking furiously. If his cousin did move into Mrs. Evans's house, perhaps they would become friends. That might well allow her to spend more time around Cameron. She would make him a good wife, she just knew it. If only he would realize it. Sighing, Sierra forced herself to put her mind back on her work. Her mother had been right. Daydreaming was a waste of time.

Three rooms and a mountain of dirty sheets later, Sierra filled her laundry bag, left her cart and started toward the service elevator. On the way down the hall, she allowed herself to think about Cameron again, her eyes filling with tears.

Joseph had been dressed for an hour before Camille finally rose. While they waited, Pa sat reading the *Chronicle* by the big bay window. By the time Camille was finally bathed and had her hair and hat on to suit her, Pa had read the newspaper front to back twice and Joseph was about to wear a path in the carpet.

As they walked down the hallway, Joseph's stomach rumbled with urgency. On the ranch, he would have eaten breakfast two hours before and be well into his morning's work. Pa rang the bell for the elevator. A moment later the doors slid open, the lacy grillwork folding like a Chinese fan. The elevator attendant touched his cap.

"Lobby, please," Joseph said as they got in.

The doors closed soundlessly. Joseph glanced at his sister. She was glowing. Pa looked bored but content enough. The elevator slowed and Joseph took a half-step forward before he realized that they were stopping on the second floor.

"Lobby, please," said the elderly woman who got on, her old-fashioned gown trailing behind her.

As the doors began to close, Joseph caught a glimpse of the housekeeper he had seen the day before. Watching her walk past, her head high and her spine straight, he fought an urge to shout at the attendant to stop the elevator. Then, at the last second, she turned to glance through the open doors and met his eyes. She had been crying, he was certain of it. Her beautiful cheeks were streaked with tears. For an instant, his eyes held hers, and it was only after the doors closed that he was able to exhale.

"You all right?" Pa asked, scrutinizing him.

Joseph nodded. "Just hungry."

Pa nodded. "Me, too. Not used to these late mornings."

"You sound like two old ranch hands," Camille teased.

Pa laughed. "We are. Or one of us is, anyway. The other one is still young and spry." He slapped Joseph lightly on the shoulder as the elevator came to a stop again, and the doors opened onto the lobby with its massive chandeliers and palms.

Camille decided that she was going to love eating in a restaurant every morning. Joseph and Pa looked bored and dull-eyed sipping their coffee, but she felt excited over nothing.

Pa was glaring out the window. The sun had come up this morning in a clear blue sky—the fog had lifted. Camille followed her father's gaze and saw a boy on the corner, holding out a copy of the *Examiner* at arm's length, shouting out his hawker's cry.

"I'll go buy you one, Papa," Camille whispered.

"I already read the *Chronicle.*"

"Please," she begged. "You can watch me to see that I am safe. I would love to go outside just for a moment. Please?" She glanced at Joseph. For an instant, she thought he might offer to go with her, but he didn't.

"Don't dawdle," Papa cautioned. He fumbled in his vest pocket, then produced a nickel.

Camille stood and smoothed her skirt self-consciously. It was the color of a blue sky, with a shawl ruffle that spilled from her shoulders down her back. She liked the feel of the cloth swinging dramatically as she walked. It was like wearing a cape.

The lobby was almost empty. Camille hurried across the thick carpet past the bell captain, who stood guarding a grand arrangement of trunks with silver fittings. She waited for the doorman to open the wide double doors, then went out and stood on the sidewalk, looking almost straight up at the sky. The buildings jutted upward, shaping the endless blue like canyon walls. As she watched, a thin mist curled above the buildings; was the fog rolling back in? Camille allowed herself as long a look as she dared, then lowered her chin reluctantly and walked primly past the restaurant window to the corner.

The newsboy made her a little half-bow and handed her the paper. His sleeve was ragged, the fraying threads hanging over his wrist. His hands were stained black with fresh ink. Camille wished that she had thought to ask Papa for an extra dime for him.

She turned and made her way back down the sidewalk, refusing to look into the long windows, knowing that Papa would be staring back at her if she did. In front of the wide double doors, she hesitated just for a moment, drinking in a little more of the fresh air and the early sunshine. Then she lowered her head and went in, blinking at the comparative dimness of the lobby as she stepped inside.

"At your service, Miss."

Startled, Camille looked up into the face of a young man who stood just inside the doors. He was pulling on his gloves, his deep eyes thoughtful, concerned. His hair shone brown-gold in the sun.

"I am in no difficulty, sir," Camille said politely. "But I thank you."

"If ever you are, call upon me, please," the man said. He smiled a little before he turned and went past her, pushing open the heavy doors. Camille stood still for a moment. It was the same man she had seen on the sidewalk the day before, she was sure. He was so incredibly handsome. So polite and kind. Knowing Pa would be irritated with her slowness, she stood still, watching through the glass doors as the man walked away. The doorman noticed her and gestured through the glass. She nodded and he opened the door for her. She took one last look at the sky. It was hazy now. The fog was returning.

That afternoon, Cameron stopped in front of the boardinghouse on Decatur Street and stood looking up at the shabby facade. The fog had come back in with a vengeance, and he was grateful. It was so thick he couldn't see more than a half dozen yards. That meant no one was likely to notice *him*.

A rooster crowed, somewhere behind the building. Cameron smiled, shaking his head. A regular barnyard, all right. He was only a little surprised at the disreputable appearance of the old house. Sierra had told him it was nothing to brag about. He shrugged, smiling wryly. The lovely Irish housekeeper had a gift for understatement. It was disgusting.

A voice down the block made him look aside. Two staggering drunks were emerging from the fog, arms upon each other's shoulders. The bigger man was shouting, his words slurred and impossible to understand. Cameron heard a window bang open and a woman screamed at the man to shut up. He yelled back at her.

"Lovely neighborhood," Cameron said to himself. "A regular Nob Hill." Whistling almost silently, he took in the squalor. The bay windows were all framed by boards with thin peels of paint hanging like ribbons down the front of the building.

Cameron looked both ways. The drunks were gone, and no one else was close enough to see in the fog. That meant no one was close enough to see *him*. Moving quickly, Cameron went up the creaking porch steps and stood by the front door.

The interior of the house remained silent as Cameron eased the door open. Sierra was pleasantly chatty, and he had encouraged her. Over that first two weeks' span she had told him all he would ever need to know about her. Her landlady was elderly and a little deaf, and lived in apartments at the back of the first floor behind the parlor and kitchen. The two workingmen who lived in the second story back rooms were early risers and left at sunup or before every day but Sunday. The older man in the second floor's front room was ill, a barkeep with asthma who slept like the dead until noon or later. The rear rooms were unrented on the second floor; so were the front rooms on the third. There were no other boarders.

Cameron eased the door closed behind himself. Sierra was so forthright, so trusting. She really was a nice girl, and he was sorry he had deceived her a little. But it was a small deception and wouldn't hurt her in the long run, he was sure. Not if he was careful.

Cameron listened intently. There hadn't been a sound since he had stepped onto the porch. He put his hand on the door pull and opened it very slowly. In the front room was a shabby dining table, long enough to seat the entire household, he was sure.

Stepping lightly, Cameron crossed the room quickly and started up the stairs. The boards creaked beneath his weight, but not too loudly. Glancing behind himself, he kept going, his face ready to burst into a pretense at confused and drunken friendliness should anyone appear to challenge him. But no one did.

Most of the doors were unlocked. Those that weren't were easy to pick with the little steel tool he carried in his vest pocket. They had old, worn two-prong locks. The knobs were loose, the jambs uneven with age and use. He opened wrong doors twice, discovering a storeroom stacked with moth-eaten boxes and rat droppings, and a cracked commode in an un-used bathroom. He started up another flight of stairs, remembering Sierra saying she bathed at night to avoid the workingmen—the bathroom on the floor below hers was in need of repairs.

Finally, he found the right door; Sierra's room was unmistakable. Everything was neat, clean, and spartan. One old trunk stood against the wall. A cheap spread covered the bed, and there was a faint scent he recognized. Did the pretty chambermaid steal fancy soap from the Palace? *No*, he decided, shaking his head, *she probably brings home half-used cakes that would be thrown out anyway.*

For a moment the window drapery caught his attention, a billowing, striped affair with a tucked and ornate valance. He bent to lift an edge and saw the tiny hand stitching. Had she sewn it herself? She couldn't afford to buy these draperies, of that much he was sure. Even the fabric had to have been dear.

Cameron let the curtain fall and reached inside his coat. Pulling out the packet he had wrapped the night before, he knelt beside Sierra's bed. Reaching beneath it as far as he could, he worked the tightly taped bundle up into the space between the frame planks and the mattress. Then he sat on the bed, bouncing up and down until he was sure that compressing the old springs wouldn't work it loose. Satisfied, he smoothed the spread, then stepped back.

Whistling so softly it was more breath than tune, Cameron took one last look around. It was a pity Sierra had not been born into wealth. If she had, he might have considered courting her. She was pretty enough for any man, and her demeanor was charming, if ridiculously naive. He knew he would have to end the acquaintanceship now, just to make sure that she was not connected with him. That meant, of course, no more friendly chatting when she was the one assigned to his room.

Cameron felt a tiny sense of loss at the thought. But it was only a small regret, and he forgot about it as he started back down the stairs. A few minutes later he was a half-block away, another misty figure in the fog that no one would notice or remember.

By the end of the first week, Joseph was tired of dashing from one end of the city to the other seeing this and that, following his father's and sister's whims of amusement. The night before they had been to a ball celebrating the anniversary of the Holdens, old friends of his father's. There had been an acre of fancy food and two acres of silk chiffon. The women and girls had all been perfumed, coiffed. Two girls had caught his eye. Once he danced with them, both proved to be charming and empty-headed, glancing about constantly to see who was watching *them*.

This morning, Joseph's stomach had an all-too-familiar queasy feeling as he listened to Camille's breathless plan making and his father's recitations of sights they had not yet seen. Pa was reading a list of architecturally important private homes when Joseph mentioned that he felt sick.

Pa shook his head. "Girlish vapors, Joseph?"

Frowning at the tension between them, Camille stood abruptly and went to adjust her hat in front of the long mirror. It was a wide-brimmed affair, the pheasant feathers and silk roses arranged like a bouquet. This was her fourth hat-adjustment session, Joseph thought. Or fifth.

"I really don't feel well, Father," Joseph said coldly. "Perhaps it was the oysters last night."

Pa pushed his reading glasses down on his nose so that he could look over them at Joseph. "Father is it? Now, when we are alone, you choose to be formal?"

"I apologize," Joseph said quickly. The last thing he wanted was to lock horns with Pa. It would only turn a minor disagreement into an hour's worth of arguing. Camille would sulk if he started the day out with sour tempers and harsh words. He glanced at her. She was turning first one way, then the other, arranging her ribbons and pinching her cheeks—and watching *him*, her eyes narrow and urgent in the mirror.

"I accept your apology," Pa said curtly.

"Oh, won't you come with us?" Camille pleaded from her station in front of the looking glass. "We are going to take a carriage up through Nob Hill, then picnic in Lafayette Park. The kitchen here will make picnic baskets, and the waiter said—"

"I was there when he said it," Joseph interrupted her, careful to keep his voice even and soft. "I really don't feel well, Camille. I would prefer not to vomit and ruin your carriage ride."

Camille wrinkled her nose at him and Pa cleared his throat but didn't comment.

"Camille?" Pa said after ten seconds of tense silence. "Are you ready? You look beautiful, as always."

She turned and he offered his arm. Together they went out the door, with Camille murmuring sympathies over her shoulder and promising that they would be back before dark.

Once the door had closed, Joseph bowed mockingly toward it, then went to sit by the window. The sun was brilliant this morning, glancing off the streetcar canopies, reflecting from the windows on the east side of the Crocker Building across the street.

Joseph pushed one of the side windows open, and a breeze came into the room. The smell of the bay was strong this morning, fresh and salty. He glanced idly back into the room and noticed Camille's pocketbook lying forgotten on the bed. The beaded flowers were brightly colored, nestled in swirls of embroidery. It might take her an hour or two to miss it, but she would. Whatever would she do without her comb and her mirror and powder? And when she came back for her purse, he would have to defend his desire for solitude all over again.

Joseph stood up. He was looking forward to a day without crowds or conversation—even if it meant being shut up in this room. If he could catch up to them, he stood a chance at having that kind of day. If not, they would be back, Pa irritated and Camille flustered.

Joseph grabbed the pocketbook, flung open the door and ran into the hall, slamming it behind him. He sprinted for the elevator, then stood, fidgeting, until the door finally opened and the cage stopped. He climbed on, standing apart from an older man who was riding downward, an unlit cigar in his mouth and a newspaper in front of his face.

In the lobby, Joseph ran again. He very nearly upset a trunk dolly, then almost stumbled into one of the potted palms that made the hotel seem more like a tropical forest than a brick building. He burst out the front doors and hopped to a halt, turning to look both up and down Market Street. His heart began to sink, then leapt again when he saw them. They had crossed the street to hire an open carriage.

Joseph hurried, dodging around the back of a piano mover's wagon, then racing across just in front of a produce cart. The driver swore at him.

"Camille? Pa!" he shouted, then realized what he had said. "Father?" he added, feeling foolish.

Pa and Camille both turned to watch him coming. When Camille saw her purse, her hands flew to her mouth and hovered there. "Oh, thank you, Joseph. What a ninny I am."

"Sure you won't join us?" Pa asked, tipping his head to one side. "You seem fit enough to me."

"Oh, leave him alone, Father," Camille said in a cajoling voice. She gestured at the driver, who stood waiting, the hack door pulled open. "Joseph might just want a day to himself."

Pa frowned. "That's girlish nonsense and Joseph knows it." He let Camille lead him toward the cab. She shot a look over her shoulder and Joseph smiled his thanks.

Once the driver climbed to his seat and lifted his long whip, Joseph dodged wagons and pedestrians to get back across the wide street. In front of the Palace, an automobile chugged up. Joseph shortened his stride to let it go by as it slowed in front of the entrance. As he passed behind it, he could not help but stare at the young man who was driving it. He was tall, blondish, with ramrod posture and a spring in his step as he climbed out of the driver's seat.

Joseph followed the man inside, trying not to stare openly, but wondering who he was. His clothes had an odd look and fit. Maybe he was European. For a long moment, until the man disappeared into the hallways that led to the grill, Joseph envied him. He looked like he belonged here, like he would belong anywhere on earth he was set down. He was exactly the kind of young man Pa would hope to find for Camille, Joseph was sure. Certainly he was the sort that Camille would choose for herself if she was given the chance.

For about ten seconds, Joseph considered following the man into the grill and inquiring who he was—but the whole thing seemed so laughable that he headed for the elevators instead. If Pa was willing to invest in a three-month stay in this flamboyant place, he could also be the one to chase the eligible bachelors down in order to inquire about their names and pedigrees.

Joseph got into the elevator, then stepped aside as a fur-coated woman and her little dog got in. "Third floor," she told the operator, and he nodded. The cage rose, then stopped at the third floor. The operator opened the doors. The woman went through them, and as they closed, Joseph saw a housekeeper's cart rolling past. He caught a glimpse of shining dark hair, braided and coiled, and a milk-white cheek.

He hesitated, but then, as the doors began to close, he stepped forward. The attendant caught at the lever and wrenched the closing doors back open as Joseph turned sideways to avoid getting stuck.

"Miss?" he said, lurching into the hallway. He just had time to regain his balance before she turned to look at him. Her eyes were gray, or gray-blue, the lights weren't bright enough to tell for sure.

"Good morning," he said, at a loss for anything else to say. Her skin was radiant and her hair was braided intricately, piled on top of her head like a shining crown.

"Did you need something, sir?" she asked politely.

Joseph stared, realizing slowly that she looked uncomfortable.

"I just wanted . . ." he began, then stopped. What did he want. To ask her name? To find out where she lived and if she could ride a horse?

"Miss O'Neille!"

A stout matron in a white uniform was coming down the hallway. The girl reacted instantly, standing straighter, her eyes lowering modestly. "Did you need something, sir?" she repeated in a strained voice.

"Towels," Joseph said in a loud voice. "If we could just have an extra towel or two. Room 445."

The maid glanced up and nodded, then pushed her cart away without looking back. Joseph reluctantly turned back to the elevator, hearing the scolding of the matron begin as the beautiful Miss O'Neille got closer to her. When the grillwork doors opened, he forced himself to get in. He went back to the room and waited, but when the towels were delivered, it was a sad-eyed middle-aged housekeeper who brought them.

"I asked a Miss O'Neille," Joseph told her, trying to hand the towels back. "She will bring more later, I am sure." He watched the housekeeper's face crease in a smile.

"Sierra is the one who told me to bring them. This is my floor today, Mister."

"Thank you," Joseph said politely, but when he closed the door, he laid the towels on his bed and sank into the chair by the window, staring out. Sierra. Her name was Sierra.

6

"Please, Celia?"

Celia smiled wryly. The Irish beauty was proposing a trade that would get her off work and out of the hotel by seven this evening. "Celia, I'll trade you two for one," the girl pleaded. "Please?"

Celia nodded, then narrowed her eyes. "Why? You have a crush on him, too? Half the girls think he's just Mr. Razzmatazz."

Sierra's blush was so rosy, so immediate, that Celia threw back her head and laughed. "I guess I was like you once, but it was so long ago that I can't recall it, honey."

Sierra smiled. "Then you'll trade room assignments?"

Celia nodded slowly. "Can't see why not. I have no need to get a glimpse of the handsome Mr. Slade in 322."

"I just want to talk to him." Sierra blushed again. "He's a friend of mine, in a way."

Celia shook her head. "You have it bad, sweetheart."

Sierra shook her head vehemently. "I just haven't seen him in nearly a week, and he—"

"You didn't sleep with him, did you?" Celia demanded. The instant darkening of Sierra's already flaming cheeks made her sorry she had been so blunt.

"No!" Sierra looked like she was about to cry. "I just . . . he used to talk to me every day, but now he seems never to be there and I just wondered if . . ."

"I know," Celia nodded sympathetically. "Gentlemen think of serving girls as trash, Sierra."

"I'm just worried that something is wrong," Sierra said. Celia could tell the girl was fighting tears.

"Here, take these two," she said, pulling a nub of pencil from behind her ear to write down the room numbers. "You can have Mr. Hoi Polloi and the little old lady in 320. She's easy. Then I don't have to feel too guilty about this."

Sierra looked so grateful that it was all Celia could do not to pat her cheek. "You stay out of trouble, now."

Sierra nodded. "I'm not in the kind of danger you imagine."

Celia nodded wearily. "Every woman is," she said flatly and pushed her cart down the hall before Sierra could say anything else.

As the week went on, the Palace filled to the rafters. Every housekeeper was required to work longer hours than usual just to keep up with the endless cleaning. Sierra had seen the signs on their gilded tripod stands on the sidewalk. The Metropolitan Opera was coming. Mrs. Halloran said people would travel from all over for the performances.

It seemed to Sierra that there could not possibly be more silk and chiffon in the world than already filled the hallways, but each day seemed to bring another entourage, another deluge of beautifully dressed people.

Sierra had been assigned to Cameron's room on Monday and Tuesday. It was easy to clean. Too easy— it looked as though he had not used the bed at all. Wednesday, she had had to trade room assignments once more, enduring Celia's pitying looks.

On Thursday, she had been too embarrassed to trade again, but she had some rooms on the second floor. She kept making trips back to Cameron's hall, fetching linens she didn't need, keeping an eye on his door, listening as she passed. Three times she pretended to drop her scrub brush as she went by so that she could pause and listen more carefully. Finally, around three o'clock, she waited for a moment when the hallway was empty of women in sweeping gowns and men in dark suits, then knocked on Cameron's door. When there was no answer, she used her passkey to open the door.

The room looked perfectly undisturbed. Cameron's things were in the neat order she had put them in. So he had not been here for at least four days. She closed the door, her heart aching with worry.

Finally, at six-thirty, Sierra was finished for the day. She signed out, then went back upstairs for a last look. The halls were less crowded now. Most of the guests were on their way to balls or dinners. Her heart hammering, Sierra knocked again, then opened the door and went in. Nothing had been touched. Cameron had not been there at all.

Sierra pulled in a deep breath, closing the door partway to hide from anyone walking past. She was starting to feel frantic. What would she do the following day if the room was still pristinely clean? That could mean that he really was in trouble somewhere and unable to make it back to the hotel.

Sierra stood beside the bay window and stared blindly down into the street at the festive crowds. Maybe Cameron was just off somewhere celebrating the coming of the opera along with everyone else on Nob Hill. But what if he wasn't? What if something was wrong?

Cameron had told her that he was from a fine St. Louis family. What did he know about the rough gold speculators and railroad men who drank at the saloons south of The Slot? His life had been very different from hers, sheltered and pampered. There were terrible places down there, with opium and women and who knew what else for sale.

Sierra shivered. Maybe Cameron had blundered into some saloon near Chinatown and had offended one of the important families there. There were a thousand ways for a cocky young man to get himself in trouble in San Francisco.

Sierra realized she was still staring at the bustle of carriages and pedestrians in the street four stories below the window. She blinked and almost turned away before she saw a glint of gold-brown hair as a man tipped his hat to a passing matron. Staring, she recognized the straight set of the man's shoulders and his jaunty stride. It was Cameron!

Whirling around, Sierra ran for the door, peeked both ways down the hallway and slipped out. She locked the door behind her and dashed for the service elevator. When the doors opened on the narrow hallway that ran in back of the lobby offices, she stepped out, then hesitated. Holding her breath and refusing to let herself think too much of the consequences, she turned away from the Third Street doors and headed for the lobby.

The area in front of the concierge desk was crowded with people dressed for a ball. The women were posing, standing with their heads held high, their hair perfectly coiffed, their laughter ringing out over the men's more somber voices. The double doors that opened onto Market Street were being held wide open by the doormen to let the crowds step freely toward the carriages at the curb, off to one party or another.

Sierra slunk along the wall, standing behind a potted palm, knowing that if she got caught, it could mean getting fired. She clutched her coat close, praying that no one would notice her risking her job for a glimpse of Cameron Slade.

"I will wait just a few seconds, then go," she whispered, promising herself. But her heart was beating wildly as she watched the front doors, frozen against the wall. A minute went past, then two. She half-turned, glancing behind her, then at the crowd around the concierge's desk, her breath coming quick and sharp.

There! She felt herself shiver in relief. Cameron was coming in the front doors, flipping a coin at the doorman, smiling at the world. Sierra smiled. He was swinging along, his buoyant stride and straight shoulders as strong and confident as ever. So he was fine, he was safe. She would see him again.

Sierra felt a rush of relief as Cameron paused in the middle of the lobby, slowed by a pretty girl in a plumed hat and an older man who walked arm in arm. The girl was mincing along, her chin high and her step short and dainty. Cameron glanced at the girl, which made Sierra notice her more fully. She wore a dove-gray walking skirt with a tiny bolero overblouse and tucked sleeves—and she really was beautiful.

Sierra recognized her. She was staying on the fourth floor with her father and brother in adjoining rooms. Her brother was very handsome, and had been kind and unassuming the day he had asked for towels. Sierra had hoped that he had not thought her rude—but Mrs. Halloran was death on anyone chatting in the hallways to a guest. She was always careful when she talked with Cameron, never getting more than a step away from her cart in the hall.

As Sierra watched, Cameron moved toward the desk. She was sure he was about to ask one of the porters for assistance with something, but then he turned and openly stared at the girl as she made her way across the lobby on her father's arm. Her back was arched and her shoulders thrown back in one of the most exaggerated bends Sierra had ever seen. She looked graceful and delicate, and Cameron seemed unable to take his eyes off her.

Sierra felt a hot flush starting at her jaw line and rising to crimson her cheeks. She stepped away from the wall and turned, heading for the narrow hallway past the gilded elevators that would lead her to the Third Street entrance.

"Sierra?"

It was Cameron's voice, and she almost turned—but she knew that her face was positively inflamed and that she would stammer and be perfectly foolish if she tried to speak.

"Sierra!"

He caught her just past the elevators, pulling her to a stop, then gently turning her back around to face him. His eyes were intent as he examined her. "Are you all right?"

She managed a nod. "I've been worried about you," she blurted out without meaning to.

His eyes lit and he laughed. "Why?"

"You haven't been in your room and. . . ." Sierra trailed off, embarrassed and amazed that she had as much as admitted she had been checking on him.

But he smiled at her, waving his hand as if to erase her concern. "I've been taking care of business matters elsewhere. Say, Sierra," he added, leaning closer. "Did you see that girl in gray? Is she staying here?" Sierra nodded, numb, unable to pull away. He leaned closer still. "Could you find out her name for me? Or what room she's in? She's going to be at a Mrs. Hampton's gala later tonight I think, but . . . I'd pay you something."

Sierra managed to shake her head as she backed

away. "No," she said as clearly as she could. "That's against the rules. . . ." She was fighting tears and a strange dizziness that made it hard for her to breathe.

"Sierra, is something wrong?" he asked, clearly puzzled by her reaction. He took her hand, but she pulled it free and spun around, running down the hallway away from him. She banged out the Third Street doors, nearly colliding with one of the waiters just now arriving for work. She ran on, hoping he wouldn't mention the incident to anyone or report her unseemly behavior to Mrs. Halloran.

Camille was jittery with excitement. It was Friday night—the beginning of a whole week of balls and galas leading up to the opening of the most wonderful event of the year. The entire city was anticipating the Metropolitan Opera Company coming from New York, and everyone wanted to celebrate the occasion. The great Caruso was coming, and dozens of other world-famous singers. Every member of high society wanted to be part of the excitement.

There were so many parties that Papa had told Camille they couldn't possibly attend them all. Joseph had argued for this one because it was in the Palace, she was sure. He could always slink back to their room when he had had enough.

The sun had set around seven in a haze of fog, but then the sky had cleared and the stars had come out. The carriage ride, in a long caravan of beautiful turnouts following the famous tally-ho coach of Mr. Beylard, had taken the guests all over the city, then back past the cemeteries and down through the Presidio. The women's cheeks were flushed with the cool night air, and conversations were animated.

The Palace ballroom was exquisite. Smilax garlands and fresh flowers festooned the balustrade between the dance floor and the orchestra. The white pillars that stood out from the walls were covered with a clever network of tiny lights. Overhead, the intricate painting on the ornate ceiling seemed to move with the flickering of the candles set on the white-clothed refreshment tables.

Camille turned her wrist to straighten her cuff, smoothing the wine-colored silk, then touched the creamy white lace that overlay her bodice and collar. At the gala the night before, she had learned that the young man with the curly hair had a name. He was Cameron Slade and he was dashing and handsome and a wonderful dancer. Cameron Slade. Even his name was handsome. She tried not to stare as he walked from the crystal punch bowl to the far side of the room.

"Pa says you are to dance with other men, now."

Joseph's voice startled Camille and she whirled around. He was smiling wryly.

"Why?" Camille demanded.

Joseph shrugged. "I think it's like trolling for fish. You try to drag the bait across as much water as. . . ."

Camille lifted her hand impulsively, almost angry enough to slap him. "Do you know we have been here over two weeks now, and you have been miserable company most of that time?"

Joseph shrugged. "I'd rather be back out on the ranch."

Camille touched her lace collar. "Helping the hands pull calves in a muddy barn?"

He only nodded. "I know it makes no sense to you, but I hate all this."

She watched him gesture at the room of swirling dancers, the tables with their centerpieces of iris and ferns. "How could anyone hate it? It's beautiful, Joseph."

"It is, in its way," he relented, obviously hearing the pleading in her voice. "I just like other things more."

"Father is pushing all the girls your way, isn't he?"

Joseph nodded.

"Some lovely girls, too."

She watched him nod again, his eyes straying across the room.

"Which one?" she asked, leaning close.

"Which one what?" he whispered back, teasing her.

"Which girl are you looking for?"

"Really, Camille, none of them have caught my eye. I know you are charmed by your curly-haired friend, but I. . . ." He paused as the music began again, this time a lively old-fashioned quadrille.

Camille glanced around. Where had Cameron gone? After a few seconds, she spotted him walking onto the dance floor with a laughing, redheaded girl who looked stunning in a moss-green gown.

"It's just as well," Joseph said, having followed her gaze. "Pa said you were to—"

"Dance with me," Camille insisted, taking her

brother's hand. The lines were forming. She wanted to be as close to Cameron as she could.

Joseph was frowning as she pulled him forward. "No, Camille, not a quadrille. They go on *forever* and—"

"Please," she begged him, desperate. "If we can get close enough when they change partners—"

"Camille," he protested, but when she pulled on his arm he came along, as she had known he would. If there was one thing Joseph hated more than crowds, it was making a scene so the crowd ended up looking at *him*.

The squares were forming quickly. Another couple very nearly completed Cameron's group, but Camille managed to maneuver Joseph around so that they were next in place just as the introduction music stopped, then began again, this time in earnest.

Camille was careful. She pretended not to see Cameron in the first three passes, then feigned surprise when her turn came to walk the center, swung round by every man she passed. She flashed him a smile, tilting her head, then swirled away, back to Joseph's waiting arm.

The red-haired girl was striking from a distance, but not really all that pretty close up. Her nose was a little too big and she had freckles on her chest and arms. On her face, they had been powdered or bleached out, but Camille was sure they had been there to start with.

The dance brought the couples into a straight line, alternating the men and women. *Now*, Camille thought, and she took her turn, spinning around gaily, laughing with her head tilted back. Joseph played his part better than she thought he would, lifting his arm so she could twirl faster, flaring her skirts so that her ankles showed. She refused to glance at Cameron again during the dance, or after it, when the couples stood in twos and fours, breathing hard. Joseph escorted her back, and she still resisted the urge to look at Cameron as he led the flushed redhead from the floor.

"Is he coming?" she asked Joseph halfway back to where the tables and chairs were waiting for those who had had enough of dancing for the moment. "Do you see him?" she demanded.

"Whoever do you mean—*ouch!*" Joseph stopped teasing when she dug her nails into his arm. "Yes, I see him. Yes, he is looking around, presumably for you."

Camille allowed herself a glance. Cameron was coming toward them, smiling. "You two look very practiced dancing together," he said as he got closer. "I am hoping you are the brother she has mentioned?"

"Our father has spent a lot of money trying to imbue us with culture," Joseph said. Cameron laughed as Camille introduced them. The music began again, and Camille turned ever so slightly, as though the melody had drawn her irresistibly.

"Would you mind if I stole your lovely sister away?" Cameron said.

Joseph shook his head. "She will wear me out if you don't." He was being gracious, almost smiling, and Camille shot him a look of pure gratitude. She felt lovely and breathless and she wanted the evening to last forever.

* * *

76

Friday had been terrible for Sierra. She had cried off and on all day at work, miserable and embarrassed, hiding her red eyes by looking at the floor all day long. Saturday had not been any better, and Celia had noticed, of course, and had chided her for being silly. Sunday she managed better in the morning, but the afternoon had been ruined by a glimpse of Cameron, the girl on his arm, climbing into the elevator. Sierra had forced herself to walk past without a single glance at the closed elevator doors. Sunday had been worst of all. None of the staff were getting their usual days off because of the extra guests, so she'd had to work. She had seen Cameron twice from a distance—and he had not noticed her at all either time.

On Monday morning, Sierra stared at her list. Of course! She had traded Celia rooms for almost a week to get assigned to Cameron's room. Now that seeing him was the last thing she wanted on earth, Mrs. Halloran had given it to her.

"Sierra?" Livvy whispered.

"Move along, please, Miss O'Neille," Mrs. Halloran said, loudly enough to make Sierra jump. She pushed her cart ahead, mumbling an apology, and followed Livvy and the rest toward the service elevators.

"What's wrong with you?" Livvy demanded once they were halfway down the long hall.

Sierra smiled as brightly as she could. "Nothing. Why do you ask?"

"Because you looked like you were about to cry a moment ago."

Sierra looked into Livvy's good-natured face. She

was a gentle gossip, always asking the others about their husbands and their beaus. "I just got a room I would rather not have, that's all."

Livvy nodded knowingly as they slowly moved forward in line. The elevators could handle no more than four at a time with the bulky carts. "The young man Celia told me about?"

Sierra sighed. "What did she say?"

Livvy smiled. "Just that the dashing young gentleman you've fallen for is head-over-heels for the little snippet on the fourth floor—that one with her father and brother?"

"How would Celia know?" Sierra said slowly.

Livvy smiled sympathetically. "She served a ball Saturday up on Nob Hill. They danced together all night."

"I have no real interest in what he does," Sierra said tightly.

"I suppose Celia misunderstood," Livvy said quickly as they got into the lift. On the second floor, Sierra rolled her cart out of the cage before Livvy could say anything more. She headed down the hall, determined to start at the far end. Then she heard the sound of a room door opening and glanced up. Cameron was locking his door. He turned and looked straight at her. It all happened so fast that she had no time at all to react, as he nodded politely—as if to a stranger—then walked past her. Heart thudding, she could only watch him go, his stride long and purposeful as he turned the corner, heading toward the gilded elevators that would take him to the lobby.

Sierra took a deep breath. It was obvious that she

had deceived herself completely, imagining romantic attraction where there had only been idle cordiality— or not even that. She had obviously angered him by refusing to find out about the pretty girl.

Pulling in another shuddering breath, Sierra squared her shoulders and rolled her cart forward, stopping at Cameron's door. There could hardly be a better time to clean and restock his room without running into him.

Her hand a little unsteady, Sierra turned her master key in the lock and pushed the door open. Cameron rarely made much mess. *It won't take long*, she thought, pulling fresh bed linens from the stack on her cart.

Sierra stepped into the room, her eyes stinging. It was as familiar to her as her own, almost. She had memorized his trunks, the way his ties hung unevenly on the wardrobe top, his habit of lining his boots up neatly, like many women did their shoes. She sighed, a sad, lonely feeling seeping through her. Her dream might have been foolish, but she missed it terribly. Now, there would be no reason to wake up excited, hopeful. All her days would be the same.

Sierra put the clean sheets on the bed, careful not to leave even the slightest crease. She held her chin up as she worked, whispering to herself angrily. "This is just as well. The whole thing was a silly daydream, anyway. And I knew it."

She picked up the pillow to fluff the feathers and was startled when a brown leather book dropped to the floor. It lay at her feet, open. It was a journal, she realized instantly. *His journal.* The entries were dated.

Sierra picked the book up, glancing back toward the door. She knew she should not read it, but she did anyway, flipping back to the first page, knowing exactly what she hoped to find. Perhaps somewhere he had noted that the housekeeper had chatted with him.

In the front of the book, Cameron's name was written in dark ink, with a flourish that made her picture his confident grin. Sierra turned a page, then a few more. Her eye fell on a day with a single line for an entry.

April 2. Still waiting for someone suitable to check in.

She slowed and turned the pages carefully. If he mentioned her at all, it would be in the last week of March or the first week of April, Sierra thought. She glanced toward the open door. They were not allowed to close the doors of the rooms they were cleaning. If Mrs. Halloran saw her cart and the closed door, she would be in terrible trouble. Sierra stepped back so that someone passing in the hall could not see what she was doing.

April 4th. Still waiting, but talked to Devereaux today and got what I needed to make the stay here easier. His only requirement this time is that I hide what I haven't used. It makes sense not to keep it all here, though my new banker is somewhat unusual, prettier than most.

That made little sense so Sierra flipped forward to an entry dated the fourteenth, three days before—the day of the ball Celia had served.

April 11. All is well. Camille falling nicely. She tells me her father owns upwards of three thousand acres and a cattle operation in addition to his speculations in railroad stocks and mining claims. This is the one for me, I do believe. She is pretty enough, though not very smart. Her brother seems a dunce as well, though sincere. I will be able to take it all, if I am cautious and bide my time. Esther, Cynthia, and now Camille. My third marriage will be the best.

Sierra felt dizzy, almost sick. The newest entry had been made that morning.

April 17. Camille and family leaving tonight, but will be back tomorrow noon. I will be waiting in the lobby as we arranged and will take her to luncheon. I will make sure she sees me flirting mildly elsewhere—time for a little jealousy, I think. All has gone smoothly. A pity she is not clever enough or deep enough to be much sport.

Sierra closed the journal. She felt physically ill. What if she had had money? He would be wooing her. "I would have fallen completely for his charm," she breathed. "I did!" Sierra shivered. She might have married him and lived to repent her foolishness forever.

A chasm of hurt opened inside her. She remembered herself walking down the hall with a lift in her step, singing to herself because he had spent a few moments of his time talking to her. She felt her stomach tighten with shame.

On the heels of her hurt came anger and a stab of

pity for the girl upstairs, dancing all night with a man who thought she and her brother were stupid but could recite their holdings. Gripping the journal tightly, like a snake she was afraid would strike at her if she loosened her grip, Sierra made a decision. She knew it could cost her her job. If Cameron came back tonight, he might report his loss to the front desk. She fought with herself for a few seconds, then hurriedly slipped the journal beneath the pile of clean sheets on her cart.

"You are a scoundrel and I hate you, Cameron Slade," she said aloud. "And I will ruin your plan, if I can."

7

The kitchen was filled with salty, fragrant steam from the oyster pots. The chef had made candied sweet potatoes in addition to the usual array of vegetables, and the odor of cinnamon and nutmeg permeated the kitchen and the dining room.

Teddy Simmons hung his order chits on the chef's carousel, then turned to see Charles, one of the young assistant chefs, standing beside the salad-preparation work table and smiling, his hands flecked with green from making salads for dinner. "So, do you work this shift from now on?"

Teddy shook his head. "Tomorrow and Friday I work breakfast. Then never again, I hope."

Charles laughed. "You hate mornings, don't you?"

Teddy nodded. "And people eating like pigs at a trough." He turned to the wine steward to hand him the chit for table five.

Out in the dining room, Teddy arranged his face in

a professionally pleasant expression. He straightened the snow-white linen apron tied around his waist, feeling content. After almost a year of working his way up through the ranks of the nearly 150 waiters at the Palace, he was about to get the second supper shift—the one he had wanted from the start. After eight o'clock at night there were fewer Americans. It was quieter, more civilized. The European guests knew how to spend a few hours over a fine meal talking and drinking wine, then left gratuities big enough to matter. Americans were like country bumpkins, even most of the wealthy ones. They were as pleased to eat boardinghouse fare as real cuisine.

Teddy poured another glass of wine for a young man at one table, then removed a plate emptied of oyster-stuffed mushrooms from another. A woman across the room laughed merrily. Her companions were all sharing the joke, whatever it was. None of them were hunched over their plates, eating the wondrous food too fast, nor were they ignoring it in favor of business talk. They were savoring the exquisite result of hard work and decades of experience on the part of the chef and his staff. As they should be.

Teddy turned to take the soiled dishes back to the kitchen and to check on the entrees ordered by the two romantic couples near the back of the room. One of the women was so pretty, it was hard to serve her without staring. Teddy sighed. Wealthy men so often seemed to have beautiful women at their sides.

"Theodore? Party of three?"

Teddy turned and nodded at Alfred, the dining

room host, then looked past him. *Damn. Americans, two men and a young woman.* In one practiced glance, Teddy took them in. There was a family resemblance between them. So. A father and his two grown children most likely. Very clearly monied, and just as clearly without even a semblance of real sophistication. The girl was pretty, but gawking about like an orphan child taken into some grand place. She was in awe of everything from the carpets to the chandeliers. No, Teddy corrected himself, watching her. She was looking at the other tables, at the other women's gowns and hats and shoes.

Teddy nodded, half-bowing, and gestured into the dining room as though it were his home and he was welcoming guests. "Please choose any table. I will be with you in a moment."

"Thank you," the older man murmured, then turned back to his son as they walked toward the far wall. "I want you to come along," he was saying.

Teddy couldn't hear an answer, but the younger man shook his head, his eyes angry.

Teddy turned before they could notice him watching them. Of course. A table of Americans, and they were arguing. He started back toward the kitchen, consoling himself. This wasn't so bad—only one table of Americans in almost two hours. With luck, he could stay on this shift forever.

Sierra awoke early—before the train whistle or the first sleepy crows from Mrs. Evans's rooster. She got up, shivering, and peeked out her window. There was no fog this morning. She could see a few lights off toward the financial district.

She lowered her drapes, less uneasy than she had been the night before. She might not lose her job. Cameron might not report the book missing, since he would be ashamed of what was in it. And the girl's family might not report finding it because of the information it contained.

Sierra crept around her room, dressing quickly by candlelight, then made her way downstairs, buttoning her coat. She would never have known that Camille and her father and brother would be gone today if it hadn't been for Cameron's journal entry. It seemed too perfect . . . Cameron's own ruin was possible this morning because he had recorded that one entry.

Sierra lit a match and held it up to read the tall clock in the front room. Four-thirty. Perfect. She would have to go in the service doors, but once inside, she could take the service elevator up to the fourth floor, use her key to put the diary under Camille's pillow, then be back down to join the others in line before Mrs. Halloran got there.

If anyone noticed her coming out of the elevator, she would say she'd left her pocketbook in one of the upper floor stock rooms the night before. It was true. She hadn't wanted to turn in her master key the night before. She was going to need it.

Sierra eased the front door open, then closed it silently behind her. As she began to walk, she glanced skyward and saw the sparkle of stars. No fog. A sunny morning and a glorious day. Deliberately, she lowered her head and looked straight down the block, thinking.

If she was let go because of this, she would apply for a job at the new Fairmont Hotel up on Nob Hill when it opened. They might not ask for referrals or references since they would be in a hurry to staff their new hotel. She could certainly prove that she was trained in hotel work. If she didn't get fired, she would keep cleaning rooms at the Palace for another six months or a year, saving every dime she could. Then she would try to find a position in a modiste's shop. With a recommendation from the Palace, maybe a shop owner wouldn't need to ask much more about her background. Her needle work was good enough to—

"Good morning, Missy."

The man's voice startled Sierra, and she instinctively veered away from it, glancing up. He was propped against the side of a building, his eyes red-rimmed and bleary. He repeated his slurred greeting. She did not answer. Sierra saw other shadowed figures farther down the street, and realized that the neighborhoods that she walked through every morning were different just one hour earlier. The people on the streets now were not on their way to work—they were on their way home, many of them drunk and swaying on their feet.

Three women wearing revealing dresses—and obviously without proper corsets—passed Sierra walking the other way. She lowered her head to keep from catching their eyes. She knew what they were, and she pitied them and would pray for their souls, but she didn't want to talk to them this morning.

Someday, Sierra promised herself, *I will move out of the Mission district. I'll get a place in a respectable part of the city.* She hurried her steps. The streetcars wouldn't start running until 5:00. She would have to walk to the Palace today.

Daniel Gibbons rolled over in his sleep, reaching to put his arm around Sarah. When his caress fell on nothing but wrinkled sheets, he opened his eyes and blinked, patting at the empty bed as though he thought she was there just somehow hidden from him.

"Damnation," he whispered to himself, sitting up.

The argument of the night before came back to him in bits and pieces. He had been drunk. Sarah had been furious. She had threatened, again, to leave him— though God only knew where it was she thought she would go. Her father had died five years before, and her mother had become like a child in her grief. She was in a sanatorium out in Denver.

Sarah's lectures were wearying. Sometimes Daniel felt like he could join in and recite them with her. Last night, she had gone through her suffragette nonsense yet again, trying to convince herself that she could live without his protection and help. She was attending entirely too many progressive meetings down at the schoolhouse. They all were. It was time the men of the community put a stop to all this.

"Sarah?"

She didn't answer.

"Sarah?"

A hollow feeling gnawing at his stomach, Daniel turned back into the bedroom. She would never actually leave, would she? He just wanted her to tone down all this progressive nonsense to a level a man could live with. He only played poker once a week. That was not a lot of recreation for a man.

Daniel got back into bed. Sometimes she couldn't sleep and she just took a walk down the lane and came back. That was probably it. She would be home before long. Daniel turned onto his side. It was only then that he saw her note poking out from beneath her pillow. It was short and to the point.

I have gone to San Francisco to live with my sister. I will not divorce you, but don't bother coming to visit. You have ruined my name and my life,

Sarah

Daniel crumpled the paper in one hand, slowly and deliberately. She would not get away with this.

Joseph lay staring at the ceiling, wondering how long he would have to be in the city before the habit of waking before dawn left him. He was beginning to hate it. At home he would dress and be on his way out to check the pastures, ride up to Raul's camp to make sure the new blood-stock bulls were coming along, or ride into Oakland to telegraph the market in Chicago—*something*.

Here, in this grand hotel room, he spent three hours a day staring at the ceiling and thinking before Pa and

Camille woke up. He had tried rising to dress only twice. Both times, Pa had snapped awake and sat up, demanding to know what time it was, what was the matter.

Joseph considered trying to go back to sleep at least for another hour, then swung his feet to the floor and stood up. At least this morning, he didn't have to worry about Pa, who had left with Camille the night before for Napa. So he could at least get dressed, sit in front of the bay window, and watch the sun come up over the city.

As Joseph pulled on his trousers and shirt, he toyed with the idea of just going home, now, while Pa was gone and couldn't fight with him about it. Would Pa fetch him back, raging and shouting? It was the eighteenth of April. Calving was almost over. If Pa made them stay as long as he said he was going to, the best of the summer would be gone before they got back to the ranch.

Joseph stretched, then fastened his suspenders and slouched into the upholstered chair that he had dragged out from the wall and turned so it faced the big bay window the night before. The drapes were already open wide and the sashes on the side-angled windows were up. He was dying for fresh air here. The city smelled like people—like automobile exhaust and sewers and rancid cooking lard.

Joseph gripped the arms of the chair. He imagined sending a telegram to his father in Napa explaining that he was in South America mining emeralds. Or in Texas starting his own ranch. Anywhere but here in San Francisco, doing nothing but eating and making polite conversation with people who bored him.

The whole overnight trip up to Napa was for Camille, Joseph knew. Pa didn't usually socialize with cattle buyers. But one of them was young, the second son of a Chicago meat-packing tycoon. He was obviously taken by Camille, who was just as obviously oblivious toward him. But Pa was apparently hoping that fresh air, spring sunshine, and a long buggy ride would do the trick. Anything to prevent Camille from spending every waking hour sighing over Cameron Slade.

Joseph shook his head. This whole junket could turn out very differently from Pa's intentions. Instead of finding a monied, well-connected man who would stabilize Camille's wild whims and impulsive behavior, she might just wind up married to a well-heeled drifter. Cameron was unfailingly polite and respectful to Pa and very attentive to Camille, but he seemed to come from nowhere, to have no family ties. Pa's interrogations had gotten him no solid information at all. Every question about the Slade family led to a vague mention of growing up in St. Louis and being a self-made man.

Joseph yawned and leaned back. So Camille might choose a dangerous man instead of a safe one . . . as for himself, finding a wife seemed a distant possibility at this point. All the dances and lovely gowns and pretty faces of the last few weeks had spun past him like gossamer on the wind.

He liked dancing and flirting well enough, but marriage to a girl whose gown cost as much as two good bulls and a year's wages for a cowhand seemed worse than foolhardy to him. And none of these girls had really taken his fancy. All they talked about at one party was how fine the next one would be and what they were having made to wear for it! They weren't stupid or mean-hearted, and many of them were pretty. But he could tell their fathers weren't happy having a cowboy's son attending their daughters. Joseph shook his head. He just couldn't feel comfortable with the city girls or their families.

He leaned forward in the chair. The sky was brightening now. He would take a long walk down along the bay and spend the morning straightening out his thoughts. Then, when Pa and Camille got back, he was going to tell his father that this wedding-bell campaign was a losing battle.

Joseph stood up and began to pace. All the young women he had spent time with since they had come to the city were more than spoiled—they were pampered. All but Camille, anyway. His sister was the most vibrant of all of them, the least fragile. Maybe if he could find a family Pa would approve of who had raised their daughters on a ranch or a farm. . . .

Joseph's thoughts trailed off. There was an odd scratching sound from outside the door. He stopped pacing and stood, astounded, as it swung inward, silhouetting a woman's form against the low-flamed night lights in the hall. He saw a flash of her dark braids as she came in and whirled to close the door behind her.

"What are you doing here so early?" Joseph asked.

She gasped and turned.

He could barely see her face, but he recognized the sweet old-fashioned hair style that had reminded him of his mother.

"I am terribly sorry—"

"Don't be," he interrupted her. "Did they tell you the room would be empty? My father and sister are gone."

She nodded, a nearly imperceptible movement, then stood hovering just inside, one hand still on the doorknob.

"I was about to clear out, Sierra," he told her. "If you could wait just a few moments?"

"I'll come back," she said. Her voice was trembling.

"Is something wrong?"

"How do you—know my name?"

He shrugged, his eyes on her face. "That day I asked you for towels. The woman who brought them mentioned your name." He studied her. She was trembling. "Are you in some difficulty?" he asked her gently.

She took in a quick breath, and answered, but he could not hear it. Her words were lost in a long, terrible groaning sound from outside. Stunned, Joseph turned slowly to face the open windows. It sounded as though the earth itself was being wounded. Beneath his feet, the floor jolted to one side, then back. He staggered, wrenching around. The girl had fallen, and he tried to shout to her—to crawl toward her. The floor trembled like a live thing beneath him, then jolted again. There was another odd groaning sound, as if the bricks were screaming. The girl looked at him, and he could see the terror in her eyes. He began to drag himself across the floor.

8

Teddy had come into work still half asleep. Finishing after midnight the night before and getting up again at 4:30 had been hard. Thank God he only had one more day of this before he switched to the evening shift for good. His wife had pushed him gently out of bed, then risen with him to make the fire for his coffee.

He had been a little late getting to the Palace, but the others had covered for him. The coffee urns were steaming and the grills lit, giving off the smell of heated iron. He glanced at the dining-room clock. Ten after five. Still another twenty minutes before the cooks would arrive.

Teddy checked his section. All his tables were ready. The snowy linen napkins were folded. Ashtrays and cuspidors were in place. All the sugar bowls were full, their little silver spoons turned just so.

The next section over was John's. He was still fussing with the pitchers of chilled cream lined up on his sideboard. Alex and Dupre had the tables along the street windows this morning. Theirs would fill up first. People liked to watch the sidewalk traffic go past while they ate.

Teddy yawned. "John?"

He looked up. "What?"

"I'm going to catch a catnap on the back room bench. Will you wake me up in about twenty minutes?"

"Sure," John promised, smiling wryly. "Late and early shifts back-to-back are murder."

Teddy nodded, yawning again.

John laughed. "I'll wake you."

Teddy mumbled his thanks, then pushed open the kitchen door. The kitchen was quiet, and would remain so a little longer. He stretched out on the bench. He closed his eyes, then quickly opened them again as the bench began to tremble beneath him. Confused, he jumped up amid the clang of falling copper pans crashing on the tiled floor. Then the heaving floor cost him his balance and he lurched sideways, slamming his head against the corner of a wash basin as he fell.

Sierra was terrified. The nightmare convulsions of the floor and walls battered against her sense of reason. *This can't be an earthquake*, she kept telling herself, her thoughts shrieking too loudly inside her skull. Earthquakes sometimes rattled the windows a little or shook the dishes in the cupboards for a second or two. This had to be something else entirely. The chandelier was swinging in a wide circle, almost brushing the ceiling.

She struggled to get to her feet and fell again, grasping at the corner of the entryway carpet in a panicked attempt to steady herself. She could hear glass shattering, and an instant later felt a shower of the tiny shards against her cheek. Fighting the weird rise and fall of the floor, she tried to turn aside, but she could not seem to lift herself against the force that shook the building. She collapsed again.

The young man was suddenly beside her. He pulled her up into a sitting position and they held each other, managing together to stay at least this much upright. Sierra heard him shouting something, but his words were lost in the thunderous roar coming from the street. Somewhere close by there was a woman's scream, shrill, knifing through the other noise. Then— as suddenly as it had begun—the shaking stopped.

Sierra realized that she had closed her eyes; she opened them to find herself pressed against the young man's chest like a frightened child. He released her, and she leaned back, staring into his eyes. They were silent for at least a full minute. Then she watched him pull in a breath and blink.

"Are you all right?"

"Yes." She nodded, slowly, wondering if it was true.

"You're beautiful," he said, then shook his head as though he hadn't meant to say it.

Then the earth buckled and snapped beneath the building, and the nightmare began again. The big bay window shattered, and Sierra watched it fall, the glass sparkling like a waterfall.

* * *

Ben Harlan had awakened long before dawn, knowing his daughter was going to be furious with him. He looked up at the familiar ceiling beams of his ranch-house bedroom and knew she would awaken in a mansion on Nob Hill where she would be treated as a treasured guest until he returned. But she would be told there was not going to be a trip to Napa. He had left her with very nice people who knew how to keep a young, willful girl out of trouble for a few days while her father took care of business.

He had tried to come up with alternative solutions, but it had been the only way he could think of to manage a trip home without leaving Camille unchaperoned in San Francisco with that pomaded mongrel Slade nosing around her all the time—and without taking Joseph home with him. If he had confided in his son, it would have only started a whole second argument.

There had been little choice. Bigger had wired, asking him to come. Two failed wells meant changing pastures, doubling up the herd, and risking losing the grass from over grazing.

Ben sat up, letting his bare feet touch the cool plank floor. Joseph hated the city, that much was obvious, but he would get used to it. He had to. That was where the future was—not out here in cattle country.

"Joseph," Ben said to the darkness that clung in pools along the ceiling beams. "If I'd thought I could bring you along, then convince you to go back, I'd have done it." Ben stood up, easing his weight onto his left leg. It took a while to limber his bad knee up in the mornings. The house was quiet, and it irritated him. His children would soon be gone, Ben reminded himself—he had better get used to it.

An odd vibration beneath his feet interrupted his thoughts. *Earthquake*, he thought and sat very still as the vibration amplified into a tremble, then into a rocking motion that made the windows rattle in their frames. He tried to stand, but his knee gave out and he slid to the floor. He could feel the bedboard grind against his back. Rolling forward, he sprawled onto the floor. Then the shaking faded.

Before Ben could get up there was a second shock. It lasted less time, but the floor rose and fell so hard that he wondered if the house would be shaken from its foundation.

When the earth settled back into stillness, Ben stood up, hoping that Camille had not been able to feel it in the city. Earthquakes scared her.

Joseph had managed to stand up, and was trying to drag Sierra to her feet. They had to get out of the building *now*. He could almost feel the weight of the floors above them and imagined the walls buckling, collapsing. How could any structure withstand this? He could see the Chronicle Building across the street. It was weaving madly, swaying back and forth like a behemoth red-brick tree trunk in some nightmare windstorm. Just audible over the weird roaring was the rising shrill of screams and shouts from the street below. He heard a horse squeal in pain and fear.

A cascade of shattered mortar fell past the gaping hole where the bay window had been. A thunderous roaring was coming now from the street below, and the insane shaking went on. Joseph fell, twisting in midair so he wouldn't hurt the beautiful young woman who clung to his hand as if he could help her. He wished he could. He wanted to more than anything, but could not stay on his feet. Every time he tried, the earth was pulled out from beneath him.

Joseph closed his eyes, holding the beautiful girl close, breathing in the soft flowered scent of her soap, unable to do more. Gradually, the shaking subsided into a gentle rolling motion, then disappeared. The stillness was sudden . . . and it felt strange.

"Is it over?" the young woman whispered against his neck. He could feel her breath on his skin, then she pushed back and straightened up, turning her head aside. He saw a flush spread across her cheeks, and realized that he had been holding her as tightly as any lover ever would. He rocked back on his heels and stood, this time managing to pull her with him.

"Is it? Is it over now?"

"I think so." He let three seconds tick past, then four, five, six . . . then exhaled. "Oh God, I do think so."

There was complete joy in his voice, and he felt electrified. The girl lifted her chin and giggled. "I feel like I have just been born. Is that silly?" She began to cry. Then she giggled again.

"It isn't silly," Joseph said and was surprised at how reasonable he sounded. "But this is no time for tears.

We should celebrate!" He took one step to the side, laughing aloud, and she swayed, facing him as he bowed. He pulled her along in a clown-waltz, and she laughed, tilting her head back, her throat white and warm. Breathless and giddy, Joseph whirled her around, stumbling over fallen clothing, his boots crunching over broken glass. Swinging her hard enough to lift her feet from the ground, he stumbled and they sprawled sideward onto the bed.

She was still laughing, her eyes nearly closed. *Her lips are perfect*, he heard himself thinking. *As smooth as rose petals*. Their laughter rebounded off the walls, then faded a little, just enough for Joseph to hear the voices from the street again.

He stood up, sobering quickly, still looking into her amazing gray eyes, as his reason rushed back. "We should get out of the building." From the hallway, a shout rang out. There was a muffled thudding against the door, then more voices. "The lifts might not be working," Joseph said.

"I know a way," the girl answered. Her cheeks were still flushed with the giddy joy of being alive after the end of the world. Then she glanced toward the window, and he saw her pale.

"What?"

"Look at the fog. It's the oddest color. Yellowish. Or is that smoke?"

He walked to the window and looked downward. The street was invisible. "It's dust," he told her. Then he turned to face her. "You are Sierra—?"

"It's Sierra O'Neille, sir." She fumbled with her coat

and he saw for the first time how threadbare it was. She followed his gaze and began to fiddle with her buttons, lowering her eyes as she put her hands in her pockets. "And you are Mister . . . ?"

"Joseph Harlan," he said quickly. "Please call me Joseph."

She blushed again, her cheeks coloring prettily. Her braids had come free of the pins that held them in place and she was struggling to arrange them again. He gestured at the bathroom, then stepped back to let her pass, taking in the room as he watched her cross it. The walls were roughened with exploded patches of plaster. The paintings had either fallen or hung crookedly. The chandelier had crashed to the floor.

Sierra turned into the bathroom, and he heard her make a little sound of disappointment—then he remembered the sounds of shattering glass.

"The mirror?"

She appeared in the doorway, her braids hanging down her back now. "And the wash basin and the shelves. All the glass is in pieces." She looked around the room, and he saw panic coming into her eyes. There was a scream in the hallway, then the sound of someone sobbing. Sierra glanced toward the door, then back at him.

Joseph could imagine her thoughts. Her job was gone, perhaps much more. He tried to keep his voice calm as his own thoughts raced to the ranch. Everyone there should be all right, he told himself. Even a strong shake wouldn't do more than scare the stock and shift the cabin on its foundations a bit.

"Where do you live?" she asked him suddenly, as though she had read his thoughts.

"On a ranch a half day's ride northeast of Oakland," he told her. At that instant there was a thump on the door and someone cried out. Sierra got an odd look in her eyes.

"Oh, my dear God," she said in a near whisper that he could barely hear above the growing clamor of voices in the hall. "Mrs. Evans is all alone, except for Mr. Hansen." She started for the door. "My landlady. I have to get back there. I—she's *old*. She'll be frantic."

"I'll go with you," Joseph said impulsively. "My father and sister are in Napa by now. It'll take Pa hours to get back here, even if the trains are running. I'll make sure your Mrs. Evans is safe, and you, and then. . . ." His voice trailed off, and he had no idea what to say next, but it didn't seem to matter. The lovely Sierra was nodding gratefully, starting toward the door. He followed her, then reached past her to open it.

The instant he did, the screams and voices that had seemed distant through the solid wood were suddenly close. The hall was jammed with people, some shouting, some weeping, some shoving along huge trunks that blocked the way. Joseph heard a child crying. Somewhere in the crush a small dog was yapping in a steady sharp rhythm.

Joseph pushed his way into the crowd, reaching back to give Sierra his hand. She took it without hesitation, her grasp quick and strong.

*   *   *

Cameron Slade had been one of the first people out of the building. He had been awake and half dressed, intending to get an early start. He had a dozen things to do before he met Camille at noon. He needed a haircut and a shave. And he had an appointment to get fitted for another suit—which meant he needed to make a quick visit to the maid's boardinghouse to get enough homemade money to cover it—and a small gambling debt he had incurred the night before.

Cameron shook his head. He had to stop playing poker. He was going to need every bit of the counterfeit he had bought, and probably more, to pull this off. Old man Harlan had sharp eyes and he would spot the first sign of anything but genuine class, Cameron knew. He wished he could take Ben aside and assure him that he would make Camille very happy. The only thing he lacked was real money. Otherwise he was a perfect catch. And once he had backing, any one of his schemes would stand a good chance of success.

The first shock of the quake had scared Cameron. The second had made him furious. He had never been closer to realizing his lifelong ambition of becoming what he wanted to be—not a tailor's son from a little Missouri town no one had ever heard of, but a businessman from San Francisco. Once the damn floor stopped bucking beneath his feet, he pulled on his boots and his coat and headed for the elevators. Amazingly, they were still working.

Now, he shoved his way to the front of the crowd in the lobby, then blundered out onto the street, coughing in the heavy dust. He thought quickly, then set off toward Sixth Street. He needed the money packet even more urgently now. The hotel was a wreck. He pictured the old boardinghouse and kicked at a loose brick lying on the sidewalk. If it had collapsed . . . he clenched his fists and kicked at another brick. It spiraled across the sidewalk.

Cameron started down the street, stepping over a hillock of cobblestones that had buckled under the pressure of the earthshock. People were spilling from the doorways of the Grand Hotel across the street as well as from the Palace behind him. Half of them weren't dressed properly. Many of the women were crying. One or two that he passed were completely hysterical, screaming and sobbing while their husbands tried to comfort them.

Just past the Grand, a line of four men sat side by side on the curb, all silent but one. He was laughing, his eyes streaming with tears of mirth. His companions kept glancing at him, their grim faces streaked with dust.

"Hey! Hey, Mister!" Cameron felt a tug at his sleeve and he turned to see a woman carrying one child and leading another. "Will you help me, please, Mister?"

"Where are you going?" he shouted at her.

"Back home," she answered, pointing down Market Street toward Sixth Street. "I was at my sister's, but I can't carry them both and I have to find out if my husband—"

"I'll carry this one," Cameron said, stooping to scoop up the taller child, a boy with wide brown eyes and a stunned look on his face. The woman shot him a look of pure gratitude. "Let's go," he said impatiently. She nodded and gathered up her crying toddler.

Cameron led off, walking fast. He glanced back twice as he threaded a path across the street. She was keeping up. Good. He had no intention of slowing down. He walked a little faster, keeping a firm grip on the boy he was carrying. The boy was in shock, and when he came to his senses he might squirm like a fish.

The cobblestones had been shoved up in places, dislodged and scattered. The big triple-globed street lights were mostly broken. Cameron could smell gas leaking from the pipes beneath them and saw broken electric wires sparking and snapping.

A block up, across from the Call Building, Cameron heard a policeman shouting at people to stay calm. He was stopping people as they walked past, asking them where they were going. Out of habit, Cameron stepped into the street, disappearing into the milling crowd, making his way around the policeman. He glanced back only once, to see the woman right behind him.

The boy in Cameron's arms picked that instant to begin to scream and twist, crying for his mother.

"Just a minute, son," Cameron said between his teeth, wanting to get well past the policeman. "Just hold on."

"Let me talk to him," the woman said from behind Cameron.

He turned on her. "Lady, I'll help you, but we have to keep going now. I can't wait."

She reached out and touched her son's cheek and spoke a few soothing words.

"Straight down this way?" Cameron asked, jutting his chin to indicate the direction.

The woman nodded. "Yes, yes. We live at Sixth and Howard."

Cameron nodded to show he had heard her then started off, cursing himself. This was stupid. Someone else would have helped her. And she was only going to slow him down. He was betting on the old woman still being alone—and that the house would still be standing. If either turned out not to be true, things were going to get much more difficult.

He imagined himself in his dandy's suit and his fancy boots, trying to work his way unnoticed through a crowd of milling workingmen, rousted out of bed by the earthquake. Then he pictured his hidden packet buried under a ton of rotten wood and musty wall boards and he shuddered. Given the choice of what would be worse, he'd take the crowd.

The boy started crying again, and Cameron began to whistle—not to calm the child but to calm himself—a soft, almost tuneless sound buried beneath the pandemonium in the street.

Mrs. Evans had not felt the first shake. The second one had brought her up out of bed, her heartbeat a thin, pulsing thread in her chest. She was frightened, but there was a strange curiosity behind her fear. Was this how she was going to die, after all these hard years of living? An earthquake?

She lay back down in her bed, and did not even cover her face when the ceiling plaster began to give way. It hit close enough to spatter her cheek with white dust, and still she did not flinch. But she prayed, her lips moving slowly, her whisper no more harsh or hurried than on any other morning of the world. When the shaking stopped, she struggled to sit up.

Coughing in irritating clouds of plaster dust, Mrs. Evans made her way out of her bedroom, pausing only to put on her housecoat and to notice that her floor was now slanted. The house was not safe, she knew, but she padded upstairs anyway, climbing each step with effort and pain. Mr. Hansen lay still in his bed, the color of ivory, his eyes wide open. She pulled his sheet over his face and left him, going from his room to Mr. Tellidine's, then to Mr. Goshen's. They were gone, and she said a prayer for their safety and checked to see that their hearths were cold, then went up to the third floor. In Sierra's room she plucked three glowing coals from the carpet and carried water from the bathroom in a glass that had fallen into the sink but somehow had not broken. When the smoking carpet was saturated, Mrs. Evans went slowly back down the tilted hallway.

The commode was cracked and water was running onto the floor—and that was probably just the beginning of the damage, she knew. The slanted floor meant the old house had slipped off its foundation. Nearly sixty years it had stood here; now it was likely ruined forever.

Mrs. Evans made her way slowly back down the stairs to her bedroom and dressed carefully, donning three waists, one atop the other. She did not want to get cold tonight, wherever she ended up. Then she went to the backyard, going down the tilting porch steps carefully and slowly, her knee aching fiercely.

Standing unsteadily in her dusty backyard, Mrs. Evans started to open the chicken-coop door, then hesitated. If she let the rooster out with the hens, they might all take off and never come back. They were just about as scared and jumbled as they would ever be today, squawking and climbing over each other and pressing up against the wooden slats.

Decisively, Mrs. Evans pulled the latch and the chickens exploded into the yard, feathers flying. She sighed as the hens grouped themselves around the rooster, sidling close as though they expected him to protect them from any further danger. They would almost certainly be gone before dark, either lost or stolen. But she couldn't leave them cooped up. It would be a death sentence.

Mrs. Evans raised her head and pulled in a long breath of the dusty air. She couldn't smell smoke yet. But it would come. She had lived through two terrible fires, or three really, if she counted the one when she had still been a baby. Her mother had told her about it so many times it was almost like she remembered it. She had never wanted to live through another one.

Mrs. Evans started back into her house, walking in short careful steps. Maybe if she left this instant, she could outrun what she knew was coming. She thought of all the bakery ovens and blacksmith shops, the fireplaces and cookstoves that had been jolted. There were red coals lying on living room rugs and oaken floors and shop planks everywhere right now.

There would be fire.

It was just a matter of *when*.

9

Sierra could just see past Joseph's shoulder. The hallway was packed with frantic people. Joseph tightened his grip on her hand. "The elevators have to be overcrowded," he said over his shoulder. "You said you know a way?"

Sierra nodded. "There's the stairs," she pointed. "Or the service elevators—but they let out in the basement." She didn't want to get into the narrow service lifts just now. She did not want to go *underground*.

He nodded and seemed to understand without her saying any more. Sierra followed him into the hallway. There were people in all states of undress. Some wept, others were still laughing as she and Joseph had done. *Beautiful*, he had called her. She glanced back at him. His handsome face was somber now, and anxious.

He caught her staring at him and leaned forward to be heard over the noise. "Are you all right, Sierra?"

She nodded. He seemed so very kind. His wife or

wife-to-be was a lucky woman. And there was a wife or a fiancée, almost certainly, Sierra reminded herself. He was a gentleman, just like Cameron was—or pretended to be. These wealthy men regarded girls like her as trash, as Celia had said.

"Is that the stairwell?" He leaned close again to gesture.

Sierra nodded. He made his way around a pile of trunks that nearly blocked the hallway, and she followed. No one stood near them; they seemed to have been abandoned.

Joseph reached around her to open the door. There were a few people on the service stairs and the sound of their footsteps echoed. Joseph took her hand again and they started downward side by side.

Settling into a quick-step rhythm to match Joseph's, Sierra felt the journal against her thigh. She put her free hand in her coat pocket to hold it still. Maybe she should just give it to him now, and explain what she had done. But when she glanced at him, his face was tense and strained. He was probably worrying about his family, perhaps about his sweetheart or his wife. Maybe he even had children. She wished she could just ask—then chided herself for wishing it.

As they slowed behind an older couple, Joseph shot her a look, then a quick smile as the old man tenderly put his arm around his wife. Sierra felt a strange hollowness in her heart. *Why, oh why couldn't Joseph be a groceryman or a bricklayer? Why does he have to be the kind of man who will never really see me?*

She felt the stairs beneath her feet tremble, and

wasn't sure if the earth had moved or if it was simply the pounding weight of the crowd. Then it came again and she caught her breath, praying to live, willing the low ceiling to hold, afraid that it would suddenly collapse, that her life was about to end. The moments passed and nothing happened.

Joseph squeezed her hand. "Are you all right?"

She looked at him, then nodded.

"Are you really? You're very pale."

She nodded again. "I'm not hurt, just scared."

He smiled. His eyes were so intense that she looked away, staring ahead of them again, picking their way through the crowd. He held her hand tightly.

I feel safe with him, Sierra thought. Then she shuddered, remembering how she had felt about Cameron. *All right*, she promised herself. *I know how to end this little flirtation of his. If we talk at all, I won't hide anything—not the orphanage, not the years living like a wharf rat.* She crossed herself and swore the old childhood oath, and suddenly felt freer than she ever had. This man would not love her when he heard her story. He wouldn't even like her. She was finally free of her illusions.

They rounded a landing, and Joseph guided her past the people who were coming onto the stairs from the second floor. When they finally stepped onto the ground-floor platform, most of the people were turning right, toward the lobby.

"Which way now?" Joseph asked, looking down into her face.

She pointed into the long hall lined with storerooms. Joseph nodded, and they stepped out of line. He let her guide him to the door that led out into the maze of service halls behind the kitchen. She hurried, turning up the long passage that ran past the offices behind the lobby. She could have gotten out by a shorter route, but she didn't want to emerge onto Montgomery Street. She wanted to be able to go straight down Market Street to Sixth. At the door, Joseph gently held her back and went out first, holding out his arm to assist her. "Stay close to me," he said quietly.

Sierra nodded, unable to speak, staring at the dust-choked nightmare of the street. It was now full of rubble. A woman sat sobbing just outside the door. The man beside her was talking in a low, comforting voice. A kitten was running through the fallen bricks and Sierra could only stare as a child picked it up and went on, following after an old woman in her nightgown.

"It's like a war," Joseph said quietly. "My grandfather was in Savannah with Grant when they took the city. He described it . . . like this." His gesture took in everything—the roiling dust, the screaming babe in its mother's arms, a carthorse lying crushed beneath a shattered cornice stone that had fallen from the facade of the Grand Hotel across the street. Its eyes had rolled back wide open. One of its hind legs jutted up at an unnatural angle, its hock turned like a broken toy.

People were milling in circles, some silent, some screaming. Sierra watched a woman rush out of the door behind them. She ran four or five steps, then stopped, staring wildly. No one seemed to know where to go. There was a confusion of noise and dust that was almost impossible to bear. Sierra could see bluish sparks on the ground near a tumble of white stone. Of course, she realized. Electric lines were down. And there was the oddest odor in the dust-filled air—something sharp. It reminded Sierra of the creosote Mrs. Evans had out in her shed. She used it to swab her chicken coop to kill feather lice.

"Oh, my God," Joseph said quietly and Sierra turned. There, among the dazed crowds, were two longhorn bulls galloping ponderously through the rubble that filled Market Street. Whatever feedlot or railroad corral they had escaped from, they were free and dangerous now.

Sierra watched the massive animals charging toward them. For some reason she was not afraid, although she knew she should be. She stepped backward, Joseph moving beside her, his hand tight on her arm. "Don't make a sound and move slowly," he said evenly, as though she were a child. She let him guide her backward as the animals slowed where the bricks and fallen mortar were the worst. They trotted heavily past, close enough to touch, swinging their pitchfork-sharp horns, bawling in fear and confusion. People seemed not to notice them until the animals were close. Then they jumped back, startled.

As Sierra watched, a man carrying a sales agent's case started across the street in front of the animals, his head down, almost running. Sierra stepped forward, but Joseph stopped her, leaning close to her ear to be heard. "Stay back. They could—"

A bellow from one of the bulls cut him off, and Sierra held her breath as it charged the sales agent, lowering its head to hook the stunned man with one long horn. Lifting its head without effort, the bull tossed him into the air without breaking stride. It lumbered on, its companion lunging into a thunderous gallop to catch up.

Without exchanging a word, Joseph and Sierra ran toward the fallen man. A trickle of blood ran from his temple as he stood up. He was white as a sheet, but seemed otherwise unhurt. "That was a bull?"

It was a question. Sierra nodded and Joseph started to explain. Not listening, the man excused himself and started across the street—but he had lost his bearings and was going back the way he had come. Joseph shouted at him, and he turned and waved once, then went on, disappearing into the dust and rubble.

Joseph turned toward Sierra, a question in his eyes. "I have to go that way," she said, pointing at the mob scene that had once been Market Street. The idea of taking even a single step away from Joseph frightened her. But she knew she had to hurry home. Mrs. Evans might be hurt.

Joseph smiled. It looked out of place on his ashen face. "I can hardly let you go by yourself."

He sounded so polite, so *gentlemanly*, that Sierra shook her head and let go of his arm. "I will be fine, sir. I am quite used to being on my own, and I—"

"I'm sure you are," Joseph said firmly. "This way?"

Startled, Sierra nodded hesitantly as he started out, reaching for her hand. She let him lead her along, grateful that he was there, grateful that he was too polite to simply go on about his own concerns.

Since they were already halfway across the street, Joseph set them out on a diagonal course through the mounds of rubble that angled toward the towering Chronicle Building. It looked odd, Sierra thought, staring up the block at it. Before she could figure out what was wrong, the ground began to tremble under her feet again.

The jumble of voices stopped as though someone had closed a door on a riot. Joseph pulled her close, holding her so tightly that it hurt. She glanced up at the Crocker Building, then at the Grand and the Palace Hotels. The architectural behemoths towered above, them, each one made of tons of brick and stone.

The tremble rose in intensity, then subsided, and the ground was still again. All around them, people began to move and talk once more. Joseph loosened his grip on her. Then he grinned at her and she grinned back at him. It was an echo of the mad relief they had felt before, she knew.

He leaned down and kissed her forehead, softly, happily. She looked into his handsome face and envied the woman who would receive this kind of kiss from him her whole life. He smiled again, and she understood him perfectly. Death had passed them by again. He released her, and she reluctantly stepped back.

Camille had awakened with a jolt, hearing screams in the distance as she jackknifed into a sitting position.

Something metallic was rattling in the darkness above her. The night seemed to close in from all sides, and she could not understand what was happening, or even remember where she was. She cried out when something struck her cheek—then ducked sideways, falling out of bed.

The floor was heaving up and down like waves beneath a boat. She crawled along, falling and struggling until she gave up and lay still, clutching a wad of cloth in one hand and the leg of a piece of furniture with the other.

When the shaking stopped, her mind stilled with it and she could only shiver and shudder, dragging in one slow breath, then the next. The second shock shifted the floor beneath her so violently that she was rolled over and found herself staring upward into the darkness. The house creaked and moaned, tortured by the unfathomable strength of the shifting earth.

Camille tried to roll back over to protect her face, but her whole body was being tossed like a doll in the hands of an angry child. Her shoulder slammed into something, and she curled away from the pain, bringing her knees up and wrapping her arms around them, losing her grip and floundering to one side. Then, suddenly, the shock eased and the floor stopped moving.

Trembling so hard that she could not stand at first, Camille got to her feet, falling twice on things she couldn't see. Balanced precariously at last, she felt her way back to the bed and sat on the edge of it, breathing hard. She could hear people calling to each other in the darkness, but she still had no idea who they were.

Abruptly, she remembered the ranch, then the Palace Hotel . . . as her mind clicked into focus. These were Papa's Nob Hill friends, the . . . Allmans? Holmans? Something like that. Her heart was hammering in her chest. This was the worst earthquake she had ever been through. All she wanted was Papa's warm hands on her shoulders, his comforting voice. She began to cry.

"Miss Harlan?" It was a male voice, the gravelly baritone of her host. Allman. That was it. Mr. Gerald Allman.

"I'm here," Camille answered, her voice stiff and unwieldy in her tight throat. She shivered and felt a rise of gooseflesh on her arms and the back of her neck. Was it cold?

"Are you hurt?"

"I don't think so," Camille answered. She wriggled her toes and straightened her legs, then touched her face. If she had been cut it wasn't bleeding much.

"Stay where you are and I will find a light." There was the sound of retreating footsteps, then a sound of annoyance and the crash of shattering glass.

Camille was alone in the darkness. She hugged herself. Where was Papa now? She had been so angry with him for leaving, and even more so for the way he had done it—as though she were a five-year-old to be deceived. He had thought to slip off without her noticing, but she had seen the carriage go and pleaded with Mrs. Allman until she relented and explained the whole stupid plan. Mrs. Allman had not said, but Camille knew exactly why her father had done it. He didn't like Cameron Slade.

Well, Papa was safe and sound, no doubt. He ought to have made it back to the ranch just at dark if he rode hard all day—and he probably had. He would have come back to get her as soon as he was able, she was sure. Now, he would be back even sooner.

Unless, of course, the tremor had been worse to the east and the house had fallen in on him. And what about Joseph and Cameron? Had the Palace weathered the shock? Camille winced, worry crowding close, cold company in the dark.

There was the flicker of a candle in the hall. "Are you all right, dear?" came a kindly female voice.

"Yes, Mrs. Allman."

"Oh, my Lord," the older woman said, making her way into the room.

Camille shivered again, seeing what had startled Mrs. Allman. The heavy armoire that had stood against the wall the night before had somehow moved across the room—and fallen squarely across the bed. If she hadn't gotten out of the way when she did, Camille realized, it might have killed her.

"We are meeting in the kitchen," Mrs. Allman was saying as she lit a second candle and handed it to Camille. "Dress, dear, then join us please. We must figure out what to do."

Camille nodded meekly, but she hoped they had no plans to leave the city. If they did, she was not going with them. Papa would come here looking for her, she was sure. And besides, she was not going anywhere until she was sure that her brother and Cameron were all right.

The wide sky overhead was sunny and clear. Ben Harlan's black gelding was jittery, dancing like every other horse on the Harlan ranch. Ben fought the big animal around in a circle, making decisions as quick as the seconds ticked past. Bigger, his longtime friend and foreman, was about half awake. He had been the only one to sleep through the shake. Once Bigger was awake, Ben knew, he was one of the most capable cowmen in the country, but he was not quick in his thinking. This was not a time for long deliberation.

Ben stood in his stirrups and began to shout at the milling cowboys. "Jake and Stel, ride the fence line north to Jerris's place, then across to the hills. If that much is tight, come back home for bed. If not, start repairs and someone will find you to bring you some beans for supper. Or breakfast."

"On our way, Boss," Stel called out and turned his wild-eyed roan toward the gate. Jake cantered after him, fighting to keep his big gray mare from bolting. Her shoulders were already dark with sweat.

Ben scanned the remaining faces. "Jess and Able. The calf barn. If no one was fool enough to leave a lantern burning, it'll be all right, I think. After that go see the shepherd that has the herd up on the foothills—what's his name?"

"Dennis O'Malley," someone sang out.

"O'Malley," Ben repeated. "You make sure he's all

right. If he isn't, one of you stay, the other one ride that side watching for strays, circling back home."

Two more horses galloped out of the yard, and dust rose in the early sunlight—then three at once, then three more pairs. When the men were off in every direction, Ben jabbed a finger at Bigger. "You run this place until I get back."

Bigger nodded. "It'll all be here when you bring them both home. I'm just sorry I wired you at all, Ben."

Ben waved Bigger's apology aside, then turned his horse westward. He cursed his decision to separate his children and then leave them. Bigger could have handled the damned failed wells. He could have moved the cattle to different pastures.

Letting his gelding flatten out and gallop headlong, Ben sat his saddle tight, lifting one hand to settle his hat. Ben knew the truth, he just hated to admit it to himself. He got every bit as tired of the city and city folks as his son did. He'd just wanted to come home for a few days, and he'd used Bigger's telegram as an excuse.

Ben rode hard, and he was glad to be riding alone. Tears were streaming down his face.

If anything had happened to Joseph or Camille. . . .

Teddy came to slowly. Standing made his head hurt, and he swayed on his feet. There were no voices close by, but he could hear muted shouting from somewhere. He rubbed his face with both hands, and they came away bloody. Gingerly he searched for the cut and found it just along his hairline. He went to the little mirror in the water closet. It was broken, but only half of it had fallen to the floor, smashed to silvery dust. He bent forward to look. The cut wasn't bad. He turned on the faucet to wash up, and the water gushed, then failed.

Turning around, Ted saw that the towels had fallen to the floor, the shelf collapsed. He reached for one and brought it up, intending to wipe his face. Then he saw a sparkle in the fabric at the last instant and lowered it. It was full of glass shattered so fine it was like sugar. He looked up. The light fixture had fallen.

Teddy stumbled out of the bathroom and looked

around the kitchen, his thoughts spinning. No water. They couldn't open without water. So it hadn't just been a rock blast at the quarry up on Telegraph Hill. He set down the towel slowly and headed for the front door of the restaurant.

"Excuse me?" someone said from behind him. "We are asking all help to stay. We have several hundred guests who have nowhere to go tonight, and their rooms are turned inside out."

Teddy turned around to see a heavyset man he recognized vaguely. Someone from the office behind the lobby. "I have a wife and two children," Teddy began, preparing himself to argue.

"Then you must go home sir, and quickly," the man said. He turned and went out through a side door.

Teddy watched him go, astounded, then pushed through the swinging doors into the dining room. He stumbled, astonished at what he was seeing. All the windows were broken along the street. He could see frantic crowds outside, people going every which way—or just standing and staring. The noise was unbelievable. People were shouting in five or six languages.

Teddy gathered his wits and made his way out the doors. He turned up Montgomery Street and began to run. If the brick and stone buildings had come down, what had happened to the wooden houses up on Dupont Street and California Street? His wife would be frantic, he was sure, and his kids terrified.

It was hard going, zigzagging around people pulling their children's toy wagons filled with their goods, people crying—some of them hysterically. One woman sat on the curb in front of a collapsed house, weeping as if her whole family had been inside. Teddy didn't ask. He didn't want to know.

The hills got steeper, but he forced himself to keep running, stumbling to a halt only when an automobile came barreling around a corner, the driver wearing goggles and a dashing scarf. A man dressed in military clothes sat beside him, pointing and shouting.

Teddy stood, gasping for breath as the careening vehicle went past. Then he glanced down the hill at the city below. It was unbelievable. Half the town had been destroyed, it looked like. He could see City Hall in the distance. This side of the front facade had collapsed. Only the metal on the dome shone in the morning sun as usual. The rest of it looked like a giant birdcage of steel girders. He straightened, still breathing hard but about to turn and go on, when something else caught his eye.

Out in the Mission district, there was a thin plume of smoke rising skyward.

Teddy began to run again.

Sierra had taken the lead, and Joseph let her guide him down an alleyway to skirt the worst of the wreckage on Market, then followed as she cut back to the street through a narrow path separating two tall buildings. Through the shattered ground-floor windows he could hear men arguing about a damaged printing press—glimpses of the machinery told him the building housed a newspaper.

It was astonishing how fast Sierra walked, Joseph realized, how little the rubble seemed to trouble her. He had released her hand when it had become impossible to maneuver through the wreckage any way but single file. He now walked behind her, watching her make her way through the chaos as fast as any man could have done. She was diminutive, yet her stride seemed to match his own. Her white-linen hemline was darkening with street dust, but he did not once see her bend to examine it. She hadn't cried, he realized, following her around a pile of brick and mats of woven wire embedded in shattered slabs of cement. Or screamed. Not once.

Joseph found himself wondering if she could ride, but knew she would think he was insane if he asked the question at a time like this. He shook his head, admitting to himself that she would certainly have a point. But he wanted to know, desperately. He had been fascinated with her from the first time he had seen her through the door, he had just never allowed himself to consider whether he could love a woman his father was sure to disapprove of. He was pretty sure that he could. Joseph looked at Sierra's straight back and lovely neck. He wanted to know everything about her. He wanted to meet her father.

"This way," she said, half turning to make sure he had heard her. She was gesturing toward another narrow passage between two huge buildings. The side of her face was smudged with dirt. Her hair was a mess, the two loose braids disappearing beneath the collar of her coat. And she was beautiful. He stared at her.

"What, Joseph? I can go on alone if you—"

"Can you ride?" He couldn't believe he had asked. He watched her eyebrows rise, two perfect arches. She looked as amazed by the question as he had imagined she might. Then she frowned and looked straight into his eyes.

"When I was ten I passed myself off as an exercise boy. I worked for nearly two years out at Ingleside track." She paused, her chin raised high and proud. Then she took a deep breath. "I slept in spare stalls."

Joseph was shocked as much by the cold, angry tone in her voice as by what she had said. He stepped back, his left foot half hitting a brick and throwing him off balance.

She waited until he had righted himself. "I can go on alone from here," she said, in the same sharp voice. "I thank you for—"

"An exercise boy?" he interrupted her a second time, positive he had heard her incorrectly. "Are you joking?"

She was blushing, a fierce, wonderful pink spreading across her cheeks. Then she whirled and was walking fast, disappearing into the passageway. Joseph hurried to follow, looking upward, disconcerted by the closeness of the walls. The sky was a bluish-brown slit above their heads. The dust was hanging heavily in the air.

Without warning, Sierra spun around. He barely managed to keep from bumping into her, and scraped his shoulder on the building, arrested by her direct gray eyes. She stood and faced him for a long moment. "Is something—" he began.

126

"I was the best," she said deliberately, cutting him off. "The best they ever had, Paddy said. They only made me quit because he got drunk and told someone I was a girl."

Joseph looked into her angry eyes and could only nod. She lowered her head. He wanted to touch her, to tell her that whatever had made her so angry, he would straighten it out, smooth it over somehow. If she missed riding, he could give her a horse. . . . But before he could shape his impulse into intelligent speech, she had turned away from him again, the hem of her coat swinging with her steps. He hurried to catch up, distracted from the full impact of her words by the madhouse noise of the crowds, the stinging dust.

As they emerged from the narrow passage, Joseph saw a new expanse of ruin. The city around them was like a kicked anthill. People filled the streets, shoving past each other, going in opposite directions, streaming around an overturned wagon, the horse dead in the traces.

"That way," Sierra said, pointing.

Joseph took the lead again, as the crowds thickened around them, holding her hand tightly to make sure nothing separated them.

Cameron set the boy down and half-listened to the woman's thanks. She had taken him only two blocks out of his way. Her husband, she assured him, would soon be back to find them. This, she pointed at a pile of rubble that slanted from a height of about fifteen feet at its apex to a few inches deep at the curb of Harrison Street, was their home.

Cameron nodded vaguely when he realized that the woman had stopped talking. Then he walked away, shouldering past a group of people standing in the middle of the street, his thoughts on the hidden packet of counterfeit money. If it was gone, he was going to have to change strategies—and fast. Camille might pity a man down on his luck, but her father definitely would not. He cursed the earthquake. Why did something like this have to happen when he was so close to realizing his plans?

At the corner of Folsom Street, he looked back. The woman was standing patiently stroking the little boy's hair, glancing up the street every few seconds. That must be the direction her husband would be coming from. There was something in her posture, in the eagerness of her glances, that made Cameron envy her husband for a second, and then pray, very briefly, for his safety.

Cameron started down Folsom, walking as fast as he could. He glanced at his watch, then shook it to see if it was broken. Almost 6:00? How could that be? He stepped up his pace. It had been almost forty minutes since the ground had stopped shaking. Anything could have happened in that amount of time. Anything. If Sierra saw him poking around, she'd recognize him and know his name. This one at least. Maybe he should leave the packet right where it was and let the fake bills be found, if that's what was going to happen. But he hated to. If Mr. Harlan whisked Camille home and this didn't work out, he was going to need a stake.

It was then that Cameron looked up, trying to see if the houses all the way down Folsom were as destroyed as the ones he was passing—and he caught his breath and stared. A blackish pillar of smoke was rising. It was down around Fifth Street, or maybe Sixth. He looked at the piles of lumber that had been houses on either side of the street. This whole part of the city was going to go up like God's own bonfire. He began to run.

Sierra was out of breath, coughing on the haze of dust as they finally broke free of the worst of the crowds and headed toward Sixth Street. She saw other women running as well. They all looked terrified, dirty, and unladylike. She knew that she looked no different, and it bothered her. She knew it wouldn't have if it hadn't been for Joseph's hand on hers. She didn't want him to see her as dirty and common—and the fact that she cared made her angry. He would never see her the way she wanted him to, no matter what.

"How much farther?" Joseph asked.

"Not far," she answered without turning her head. "Another six or seven blocks." The words came out timed to her breaths. She negotiated the corner, turning onto Sixth, then glanced up to meet his eyes. "If you want to go back—"

He shook his head. "I'll make sure you're all right first. Then I'll go back and find my father and Camille." He looked past her, pulling her out of the way of two big men dragging a piano down the sidewalk. The concrete was ruining the carved feet of the instrument. A string of six or seven children followed the piano along, each and every one of them crying.

"Oh my God," Joseph muttered once they had passed.

Sierra glanced at him again. He was looking down the street. The rising black smoke seemed so much a part of the destruction and chaos around her that it took her a moment to understand. When she did, she turned back to Joseph. "But they'll put it out. The fire-house is right down there—between Folsom and Shipley. They'll see it."

He nodded and she glanced at the smoke again, then hurried along, lifting her skirt and coat to free her stride. The journal swung against her leg at every step, reminding her of Cameron and her humiliation at believing he had cared for her. She quickened her step again and felt Joseph match her pace.

"It's Prost's Bakery," she said woodenly, when she realized that the heap of rubble she was looking at was the place where she often bought bread for Mrs. Evans on her way home. The whole neighborhood seemed unfamiliar, strange. She looked around, her heart racketing inside her chest. Everything was different. Ruined. Most of the houses had collapsed or stood askew on their foundations.

By the time he reached the ferry, Ben Harlan was frantic. The first load of refugees were gibbering like startled sparrows to anyone who would listen. The city was a ruin, the streets were buckled, the mint was wrecked, half the financial district had collapsed.

Ben shouldered his way through them as they disembarked, then rode the little boat, his eyes glued to the peninsula across the water. He recognized some of the other passengers, but no one he knew well. Garvin Jones, a respectable Main Street saloon owner, stood next to Daniel Something-or-other—Ben wasn't sure of his last name, but most everyone in Oakland knew his face. He was a do-nothing drunk and gambler made half respectable because his wife, Sarah Mason, came of good honest stock. Ben looked around. He didn't see her, and now that he thought about it, he hadn't for a week or two—not even in church. Maybe she had finally left, gone to her sister in the city after all.

The destruction on the other side of the bay became easier to see the closer they got. As did the spires of smoke. Ben counted three. It was hard to tell exactly where they were coming from, but he kept trying anyway.

As the ferry breasted the choppy waves in little lurches, the conversations around Ben wilted into a tense silence. The passengers all stared at the city that had been a white and shining beauty a few hours before.

Cameron reached the boardinghouse out of breath and sweating. He ran up the steps and called out once before going inside. The building was askew on its foundation, and Cameron had seen enough collapsed houses in the neighborhood to be grateful that was as far as the damage seemed to go.

He took four quick strides across the front room,

then turned to go up the stairs, moving as silently as he could. At the top of the first flight, he glanced back down, daring to hope. So far, so good. He went upward again and knocked softly on Sierra's door, waiting until he was sure she wasn't inside before he pushed it open.

The beat-up armoire had fallen, and the bed had been jounced from the wall and sat at an angle across the center of the room. The window was broken; glittery crescents of glass stuck in the gaudy curtains.

Cameron ran to the bed and lifted it, grunting as he tipped it onto its side. His packet of papers was still there, jammed tightly between the slats. He freed it and turned to leave.

"Hold it right there, young man," said the old woman standing in the doorway. She was pointing a pistol at his chest. Cameron felt sweat spring out on his forehead. Then he smiled.

The old woman cocked the gun.

11

Camille sat at the dining room table. The Allmans were devising a plan of action. Camille only half-listened, staring out the window that looked out over what had been San Francisco's beautiful downtown. Now it overlooked a smoking ruin. The glass in this window was intact, but the bay window in the front room had been broken and was now letting in distant screams and shouts and the unceasing barking of frightened dogs.

Camille stood and walked to the window to look down to the street. The sidewalks were filling with people. Carriages were lined up along the curbs. Chinese houseboys were running back and forth carrying trunks and packing boxes. Camille tried to feel the excitement and agitation that everyone else seemed to be feeling. But she couldn't. She felt an eerie kind of calm instead, as though there were a pane of protective glass

between herself and the panic, the fire—the earthquake itself.

"Camille will come with us, then?" Mrs. Allman was
saying.

Her husband nodded. "Unless Ben makes it here in
the next few hours and decides differently. We can
leave word with Lee, and we can leave a note on the
door. I'll cable him in Oakland from Sacramento when
we get there just to be sure."

Camille didn't turn from the window as she listened.
But she was making a decision inside the strange silence that filled her heart. She was not going to go
anywhere with the Allmans. If Papa didn't come, she
would go alone to the Palace Hotel and find out what
had happened to Joseph and Cameron. Cameron
would be there waiting for her if he was alive, of that
much she was sure. So would her brother.

"Camille?"

"Yes, Mrs. Allman?"

"Come away from the window, child. It's unseemly
to watch like that. People are barely dressed and
hardly at their best."

Camille turned, her eyes lowered. "Yes, Mrs. Allman." She left the dining room and walked back to the
bedroom she had slept in and closed the door. This
window faced Chinatown, and she could see the rows
of collapsed wooden buildings in the distance.

She had never been to Chinatown. Papa had always
said there were things there a girl should not see.
Prostitution, he had meant, and probably the opium
dens she had heard about. But other people had gone

there and come back with wonderful descriptions of exotic, beautiful women, shops full of herbs, and savory food. Now she would never see it, Camille knew. It was gone.

She saw faint spirals of smoke rising from the wreckage, but that didn't bother her. San Francisco was equipped with one of the best and most modern fire departments of any city anywhere. It wouldn't be long before they had the fires out. But then what? Where were all the people whose houses had collapsed and been ruined going to go?

Maybe Papa would let Cameron come stay at the ranch for a while, until he sorted out what he was going to do next. Maybe, Camille heard herself thinking, they would decide to marry, a "whirlwind affair," as the papers called it when it happened to tycoons or famous stage entertainers. She smiled. A whirlwind affair, and then a wedding.

Camille still felt the odd calmness surrounding her, insulating her from the ruin of the city. It wouldn't be long before Papa came. They would go find Cameron and Joseph. Then they would all go home.

Joseph could hardly believe what he was seeing. Every block led them into worse ruin and more fires. The streets here were blocked off with shattered wood and tumbled foundations. The destruction was very nearly complete. And the human wreckage was almost more than he could bear to look at.

There were people dead in the piles of splintered boards and slabs of plaster and roofing tar. Here and there he could hear the screams of some poor soul trapped under tons of lumber and stone. He did not call Sierra's attention to these cries, but he knew she had heard them when her hand tightened on his.

The people on the streets were a mixture of work-ingmen and their families and the sort of people that one never saw in the daytime. There were women who might be tavern entertainers—sad-eyed, hard-faced women; and a few younger ones, still pretty but with a sullen anger in their bearing and eyes that made him want to insist that Sierra turn around and leave this place now, to protect her own goodness.

But she seemed less shocked than he was as they walked. She politely excused herself to undershirted Irishmen and Italians who eyed her quickly if their wives were nearby and more slowly and carefully if they were not. She exchanged nods with the slattern girls in her path and the old rheumy-eyed alcoholics who sat hunched along the curbs.

He was about to ask her how much farther they had to go when she raised her hand, lifting his with it, and gestured. "Thank God it hasn't collapsed."

Then, she let go his hand and began to run. He had to sprint to catch up, marveling again at how well she picked her way through the broken cobbles, fleet as any deer. He slowed to let her lead through a nar-row place where the street itself had sunk on both sides. Running behind her he saw that her braids were coming undone. Her hair was as beautiful as the rest of her.

A gunshot startled Joseph; Sierra stumbled to a stop.

"Which house?" he asked her. She pointed. "That's where the shot was, I think."

She nodded and then started forward again, walking slowly, her head tipped to one side, listening.

"Sierra?"

"Shhh."

He could see her trembling, and he tugged at her sleeve. "I'll go look."

She shook her head and kept going. He followed her to the door, then pulled her gently aside and went in first. There were no voices, no footsteps, no sounds at all.

"Mrs. Evans?" Sierra called.

There was no answer.

"Mrs. Evans," Joseph shouted.

"I'll check her room," Sierra said, and he let her lead the way, glancing around for something he could use to defend them if he needed to. Passing the front room fireplace, he picked up a poker and held it close to his side.

Sierra pointed at an open door, and they advanced toward it slowly. The room was empty. The bed stood in the center of the room. A tall old dresser had crashed forward. There was broken glass of a hundred different colors on the bare wood floor.

"She collects little painted figures. Cheap ones from the bric-a-brac places," Sierra said.

Sudden footsteps pounded on the stairway and Sierra whirled, but Joseph caught her arm and ran ahead of her back down the little hall to the front room. A man was coming down, his face averted, one arm up as if to shield himself from a blow. Joseph heard Sierra gasp. The man cursed as he leapt the last six or eight steps and sprinted for the doorway.

"What are you doing here?" Sierra cried out, but the man didn't answer. He was out the door and down the steps before Joseph could react.

"That was Cameron Slade," Sierra said slowly.

"My sister's suitor?"

She nodded slowly, her face a confusion of emotions. Joseph stared at her. "Do you know him? Why would he be here?" Sierra shook her head without answering, then started up the stairs. Joseph could only follow her as she climbed straight to the third floor and stopped in the doorway of a room that he instantly knew was hers. It smelled of the same blossom-scented soap he had smelled on her skin.

"Sierra?"

She still wouldn't answer him. She was staring at the fallen armoire. Her bed had somehow landed on its side, and the bedding was sliding off it. As he watched, her pillow slumped toward the floor, then dropped as the blanket fell away. Sierra was staring at it. Joseph could almost read her thoughts in the quizzical expression on her face. Why was the pillow falling *now?*

Sierra walked around to the far side of the bed, almost tiptoeing. He watched her, the poker gripped tightly in his hand. She stopped suddenly, staring at the floor. Her face went white. Joseph took three quick steps around the end of the bed. An old woman lay on the floor, her eyes staring sightlessly at the ceiling. She had a pistol in one hand. There wasn't a mark on her.

"Mrs. Evans," Sierra whispered, "Oh my God, no." Then she turned and ran down the stairs. Joseph followed. Without warning, she stopped halfway across the front room, dropping to her knees. She began to cry. Joseph knelt beside her and put his hand on her shoulder. He could feel her whole body shaking beneath his fingers. He stayed quiet; he had no idea what to say to her. He remembered crying like this only once in his life, alone behind the barn after his mother had died. He had no idea what he ought to do, but he knew what he must not do. Interrupting her would be wrong. So he sat still, silent, his hand on her shoulder, waiting.

Sierra's sobs gradually drew farther apart and he could hear her taking quick breaths between them. Finally, after a long time, she seemed to feel his hand on her shoulder and she turned and hid her face against his chest.

"She was like a grandmother to me, like . . . family," Sierra said slowly.

He stroked her hair away from her tear-soaked cheeks and rocked back and forth slightly, aching inside. He would have given anything to take her pain away. He held her close as she began to cry again, slower and softer this time.

12

The ground was shaking again. Teddy cursed the feeling. He had lined up his wife and three children in front of the children's wagons stacked with trunks and boxes. "We are going to your uncle Val's," he announced, ignoring the tremor. There had been dozens of shocks since the big one and even the children had stopped reacting.

"I don't want to go," Salvatore whined.

Teddy glared at his son. "You are almost eleven. Be a man. You are upsetting your Mama and sisters."

"But Scuffy is gone," Sal said, sniffling.

"He is a dog, Sal," Teddy said flatly, angry at his son for acting like a baby at a time like this. The girls were holding up better than he was.

"But Papa—"

"But Papa nothing," Teddy said. "Now, what did I tell you?"

"We are to hold hands and stay together no matter

what," Mary said, reciting like it was a piece she had gotten by heart for school. "And we listen to you."

"To every word," Teddy said. "I don't want to lose any of you in the crowds."

The girls nodded, but Sal was still looking around for the damn dog. Teddy reached out and thumped him lightly on the top of his head. "Did you hear?"

Sal grimaced. "I heard, Papa. But—"

"No more talk about the dog. Every restaurant in town has fallen down. The coolers and storerooms are full of food. The Palace alone could feed a hundred dogs for a month."

"Did the whole building fall down, Papa?" Mary asked, wide-eyed, and Teddy cursed himself. He should know better than to exaggerate in front of Mary. If she had been a boy, she'd have made a good priest. No one could ever get anything past her.

"No," he said, leveling with her. "But plenty of other buildings did. Especially the wooden ones. I've told you all this ten times."

Teddy looked up. Other families were walking along the sidewalk. Everyone was afraid of the fires now.

"I'm thirsty," Teresa said quietly.

Sal made a face to tease her. "The faucets don't work, remember?"

"I know," Teresa said, "but I am really—"

"We'll all get a drink soon enough," Teddy told her, picking her up to sit her on his hip. He glanced at his wife. Anna hadn't said a word in an hour. Her face was sweaty and her eyes were empty. "Shall we get started?" he asked her.

She didn't answer him, but she bent to pick up the wagon handle. He knew she still wanted to stay, and he'd been humoring her for hours, but in his heart he knew they should leave.

"All right then," Teddy said, trying to sound cheerful. "Let's go see Uncle Val. We'll call him from the phone in the ferry building on the Oakland side."

Mary narrowed her eyes. "What if Oakland is as bad as here?"

Teddy looked at the sky, then at the elm tree that leaned at an angle out over the street. It had broken the wires, but hadn't fallen all the way to the ground. "It's not bad over there at all," Teddy said, still without looking at his daughter. "Hold hands now. Here we go."

Camille stood at the dining-room window again, watching the smoke-shrouded city below her. She listened to the intermittent explosions that Mr. Allman had told her were intentional, set by army engineers and firemen trying to make firebreaks to control the spread of the flames. The late-afternoon sun was shining at a slant through the smoke, tinting everything a dirty pink. She could hear the Allmans directing their staff, going through the motions of an evacuation. They were packing their most precious things, deciding what to leave to possible looters.

"The city is going to burn," Mr. Allman kept saying. And his wife responded every time with, "Oh, dear my God in heaven, keep us safe." Camille felt like screaming at them both to be quiet.

"How are you doing, dear?" Mrs. Allman said from behind her.

Camille jumped, startled.

Mrs. Allman was instantly apologetic. "I am so sorry, dear. All our nerves are a bit raw, I suspect."

"How much longer before you are ready to leave?" Camille asked. "I will want to go by the Palace first to meet my father and . . . my father should be there now."

Mrs. Allman was shaking her head. "Gerald says we will go out of town to the north now. That whole part of the city is aflame, dear. We'll leave word for your father here and wire him the instant we can, dear."

Camille nodded blandly, waiting for the kind and frightened Mrs. Allman to leave the room. Then she went back to her bedchamber and began packing her things. Her window wasn't far from the ground. She would leave the Allmans a note.

Sierra wasn't entirely sure when she had stopped crying. Joseph had not moved, other than to keep stroking her hair. He seemed content to sit, holding her, waiting for her to finish crying.

"I am so sorry," she managed finally, sitting up. She was acutely aware that her cheeks were dirty and blotched and that her eyes were swollen. She looked aside.

"You have nothing to apologize for."

"You must think me a perfect mess," she said, trying to sound like the young women she had passed a hundred times in the halls of the Palace Hotel. "You must think—"

"I think you are remarkable," he said quietly. "And beautiful."

She could only stare at him. His eyes were on hers, his expression intense and direct. Sierra felt something deep inside herself unfold, then close again. Mrs. Evans always said that men loved danger, whether it was the gold fields or war or betting big stakes at a gambling table. Joseph was probably just aroused by everything that had happened, his judgment clouded. Sierra knew it was true. A lot of the housekeepers said similar things and—

"When all of this is over," Joseph was saying slowly and deliberately, "will you see me? I mean, could I call upon you?"

"Your father won't like it."

"What about yours?"

She tried to keep her face smooth, emotionless, but he must have seen the pain pass through her eyes because he suddenly took her shoulders and pulled her closer. She was stiff and frightened in his arms. "My parents died when I was seven," she managed to whisper. "I have no family at all."

"Sierra, I . . ." he began, then he fell silent and kissed her. His mouth was warm and soft . . . then, for an instant, the kiss changed from tender to fierce. She opened her eyes, breathless. A feeling she had no experience with was blooming inside her like a rose after rain. Joseph was still staring at her, looking into her eyes. Without quite knowing that she was going to do it, she kissed him back.

It was Joseph who finally ended the second kiss, but

held her tightly for a long time before he leaned back to look into her face. "We have picked the worst night of the world to do this."

She smiled, not sure she could trust her voice—or anything else. "To kiss?"

"To fall in love," he said. "You insult me, miss. Do you think you can toy with my affections?"

She laughed as he got to his feet and went to the door and flung it open.

"Sierra?"

She heard something in his voice that made her scramble to her feet and go to stand beside him looking out. The street was hazy with smoke now and she could see flames less than two blocks away. There was a muted percussive sound, unlike anything she had ever heard.

"Dynamite," Joseph said instantly. "They're blowing up something, or the fire has found a powder shed."

Sierra looked up the street to see a line of soldiers marching through the smoke. It was eerie—as though war, not earthquake, had descended on her city.

"Are they blasting on purpose?" Joseph yelled out to the men.

One of them turned and cupped his hands around his mouth to shout back. "Trying to make a firebreak somewhere up around the Mint, up above The Slot."

Joseph nodded his thanks, then turned to Sierra. "Get whatever you want to save."

"But Mrs. Evans . . ." Sierra said, barely managing to speak around the painful tightness of emotion in her throat. "She always said she wanted to be buried in the cemetery north of here. It's grassy, and there are trees and . . ."

"We don't have a choice, Sierra. She wouldn't want you to die trying to make sure she got the burial she wanted, would she?"

Sierra shook her head, knowing he was right. "Help me, Joseph," she asked in a tiny voice. She wasn't sure he could have heard her, but he turned.

"I will. Tell me what to do."

Sierra looked into his eyes for a second before she could answer. "I just want to move her downstairs. We could just put her in her own bed, not on the floor like that and—"

"Of course we can," Joseph said quietly. "But we need to hurry."

Sierra nodded and swiped at the rising tears in her eyes. Then she led the way up the stairs. Cameron's journal bumped her thigh with each step, and she wondered again what he had been doing here. If he hadn't come, Mrs. Evans would still be alive—of that much she was sure.

Sierra tried to think clearly. She would take her mother's small silver hairbrush and her father's little prayer book. She would have to leave the old trunk and the rest of what was in it and hope that the fires would spare the house until she could come back. She wrestled with the tangle of feelings inside her as she went up the next flight of stairs. She could hear Joseph's footsteps behind her, solid, steady, and close.

*   *   *

"Get back!" the ferryman was shouting. "Stand clear!"

No one listened. The crowd pressed closer, mothers with one hand on a trunk handle and the other pulling first one child closer, then another.

Ben Harlan looked out at the solid wall of faces and wanted to break a way through with his fists. How stupid were these people? How frightened? Couldn't they see that unless passengers could get off the ferry, they couldn't get *on?*

The ferryman climbed up on the rail so that people farther back on the dock could see him. "Make room!" he yelled, motioning like someone shooing a pesky dog. He shouted twice more, but the crowd held its ground. No one wanted to give up so much as an inch, in case their neighbors in the line didn't follow suit.

"Oh, for Crissakes," the ferryman said in disgust, climbing down. "All the trips we have taken since daybreak and they're still afraid this'll be the last one." He stared at the upturned faces.

Fed up with the frantic crowds that had cost him half a day's delay on the Oakland side and another two hours at the ferry dock, Ben pushed his way forward and cupped his hands around his mouth. "Let us through!" He pointed, jabbing an angry finger at the crowd. Then he pushed his coat back, drew his pistol, and made sure everyone saw him raise it to the sky. "Let me through!" he bellowed, and shot straight up into the air three times.

A little path opened at one side of the crowd. Ben holstered his gun and started through it, the other fifteen or twenty passengers following close behind.

"Thanks, Mister," a man said from somewhere off to his right. Ben nodded curtly, not even sure who had spoken. This was the danger, he thought as he stepped from the dock up onto the planked terrace of the ferry building. People were going to panic and do stupid things—and God pity anyone in their way at the wrong time.

As he elbowed his way through the throngs, Ben thought about Camille's trusting nature and Joseph's willing heart and he grimaced. At least Camille was with the Allmans, and if they evacuated she would go with them. Still, he thought, it might be best to make sure she was all right before he went looking for Joseph. Ben shook his head, wishing he had never lied to either of them. He prayed he had not increased their danger.

There were none of the usual carriages or hacks parked by the low curb in front of the ferry on this terrible day. Just beyond it, where the cobblestones had risen up the gentle slope toward Market Street, there was now a five-foot drop where they had collapsed into a chasm. Making his way through white-faced, exhausted-looking crowds, Ben scrambled up it and went on. He glanced back once. The ferry building tower, with its huge clock face, was badly damaged. The sandstone that the masons had faced it with was cracked and broken. Then Ben realized that the great clock still stood at 5:12. Had that first dawn-hour shock stopped it?

The streets were choked with people, bicycles, carts, and wagons. Every kind of conveyance was lined up, headed the other way, as Ben began walking toward the smoke. He passed a family pulling a ponycart full of bedclothes, books, and the whatnots women all seemed to think were so important. The wife was weeping loudly, tears running down her cheeks, her wailing shrill and ceaseless. A second woman, much younger, caught Ben's eye. At least this woman wasn't crying as she drew her children's toy wagon along. Her daughter, riding astride her hip, looked as grimly determined as her mother did. Her husband walked staunchly beside her, pulling a second wagon. In it sat a young boy, red-faced and wailing, and another little girl.

As they went by, Ben looked into the face of the father a second time. There was a light of recognition in the man's eyes, too, but he said nothing. It took Ben a block more, weaving through the endless crowds, before he placed the man. It was the waiter who had served them breakfast a dozen or more times. He seemed a good man, hardworking. Ben wished him well.

Ahead, the buildings of the financial district were ablaze, the air thick with smoke. With every step the crowds were thinning. Very few people were coming straight up Market Street now. A soldier appeared out of the acrid fog and gestured with his rifle, directing Ben to turn northward at the next corner. Ben followed the man's directions, coughing on the smoke, trying to keep his sense of direction as he went up Sacramento Street. He didn't want to go farther than he had to this way before he turned toward Nob Hill.

He could see glimpses of the grand homes and tall trees when the wind thinned the smoke for a few seconds.

Two soldiers nailing a poster to a saloon wall caught Ben's attention a moment before he smelled the stench of spilled whisky. Broken casks and barrels were scattered in the gutter and across the sidewalk. As the soldiers walked away, Ben stopped to read the notice. All liquor in the city was being destroyed by order of General Funston. A second handbill announced that looters would be shot on sight. That order was from the mayor, E.E. Schmitz. Ben shook his head. *An order to kill on sight from a mayor? Could it be legal?* Destroying the liquor made sense, to keep the peace. But the saloon-keepers would be furious, he was sure.

Stumbling over a tangle of dirty blankets lying on the cobblestones, Ben cursed himself. This was no time to twist his bad knee and cripple himself. Camille needed him and, perhaps, so did Joseph. The street looked like a scene from hell, and Ben began to pray for the safety of his son and daughter.

Camille was pacing like a Barnum lion. Her satchel had been packed for hours. It would soon be evening, and the Allmans were still dithering and dickering about what to take and what to leave. Camille had wanted to wait for them to leave so that she could be sure they were on their way to safety—and be sure that they would not try to pursue her—but the whole day had passed while they carried and sorted, and now Camille overheard them talking about staying the night.

The idea of waiting another few hours for it to get dark infuriated Camille. If Papa had arrived, she would at least know that Joseph was all right. And he probably was. Mr. Allman had brought her word from a passerby that the Palace had not collapsed, that the guests were uninjured, if terrified. But, thanks to Papa's little scheme of pretending they were going to visit Napa, she was pretty sure that Joseph had no idea where she was. So he would wait at the hotel, watching and hoping that she and Papa would soon arrive.

The fire had spread through downtown, but it had roared through the cheap wooden houses south of Market. Camille could see the gutted Call Building from the window. It was impossible to tell how bad things were that far away. Maybe most of the fires around the Palace were out. She would at least start there. And if she couldn't find Joseph or Cameron, she would just come back to the Allmans'.

Camille slid up the window sash and looked out. The ground was farther away than she had thought. She stood uncertainly, glancing at her closed door and hoping that neither Mrs. Allman nor her husband would choose this minute to come and check. Then she whirled around and fished through the escritoire drawers until she found pen and paper. Leaving a note apologizing for her behavior seemed only polite, but it was hard to control her trembling hands. Now that she had decided to slip away, she could hardly stand to wait.

When she stood back at the windowsill, she hesitated once more, measuring the distance down. Every other novel she had ever read described someone going out a window. Girls went to meet their lovers, boys escaped their fathers' anger, runaways left home. "And I will break a leg trying," she thought wryly as she lifted one foot and swung it over the sill. She straddled the sash, her dress hiked up above her knees. She tossed her satchel over and heard it hit the ground. It wasn't that far. She had climbed trees five times this high as a girl. *But not*, she admitted to herself, *in a tight-laced corset*.

Camille turned, rolling onto her stomach, then wriggled backward to let herself slide downward, her hands gripping the stone windowsill. When she let go she dropped about four feet and stumbled backward awkwardly, sitting down hard on the grass the Allmans had planted to keep down the dust.

Cameron was sick with the heat and smoke. The crowds were nearly impenetrable, people moving along at a snail's pace. The explosions were closer now. Someone had explained to him what the firemen were doing and he was desperate to get out of the path of the blasting, but it was impossible. The crowd flowed like a human river between the curbs.

When he could finally see the tall buildings along Market Street again, he could also see flames pouring from their highest windows. An old woman fell in front of him, and he helped her up, then released her into the arms of her elderly husband, who thanked him warmly.

Cameron cringed, his stomach weak, remembering

how the old woman in the boardinghouse had suddenly slumped against him. It was at least the twentieth time he had relived the scene, and his own weakness was starting to make him angry. She had said she would shoot. He had not meant to harm her. It *wasn't* his fault.

Coming back through the Mission district had taken him two or three hours, he was sure. The smoke was terrible and his lungs ached, but he was wary of just setting off on a side street. He wanted to get back up onto Market. It was the widest thoroughfare in the city, second only to Van Ness Avenue. If the ground shook again, he would at least have a chance of dodging the falling brick and stone.

Cameron was shoved from behind, and he cursed the crowd under his breath. He knew where they were all headed. They wanted to go straight down Market to the ferry, somehow believing there would be room enough for all of them with their trunks and wagons and carts.

At the next intersection, soldiers were standing across the road, shouting and gesturing. Following their signals, the throng was turned away from Market and headed up another narrow street.

Pushed along against his will, Cameron managed to work his way to the edge of the street and ducked down an alleyway. Standing still, he tried to think of a way to salvage his plans. Why the chambermaid had been with Camille's brother was anyone's guess. But Sierra had seen him in the boardinghouse, of that he was sure. She had met his eyes, had almost shouted out his name. And she would tell Joseph.

Stepping through a pile of sharp-edged masonry that had been jolted from a decorative wall, Cameron headed back toward Market. His best chance of escaping Ben Harlan and the law was to leave now, somehow, and to put as many miles between himself and this ruin of a city as he could. He would get his clothes and his journal if he could, and then he'd head for the train. He patted his suit pocket to make sure the money was still there.

Staying close to the buildings and walking fast, Cameron cursed when the ground trembled beneath his feet, as it had done so many times since that morning's shock. He could not keep himself from stopping and cowering, but the shock was short and weak and he went on.

The streets were almost empty here. The soldiers were directing people around the worst of the fire. Engines stood in the street and soldiers marched past, their captains shouting orders that Cameron wasn't able to understand over the roar of the fire and the clatter of an automobile engine. As he watched, a dashing man in driving clothes wheeled around a corner and headed up Fourth Street, a man in military garb beside him.

As he came within sight of the Palace Hotel, the ground shook once more. Cameron glanced up at the Crocker Building, then back at the Palace. There were flames flickering in the windows of both buildings. The shaking stopped and he lowered his eyes. It was only then that he saw Camille, her eyes wide and frightened, running toward him through the smoke.

13

The grounds of the Protestant Orphans Asylum were filled with people standing in the open, most of them staring out at the flames and smoke on the other side of Mission Street. So far, none of the buildings on Laguna Street were afire. Only the saloon across the way with its huge, neatly painted sign announcing Wilson Whiskey looked damaged—and the soldiers had done that. The barrels were all broken now.

Sierra looked up at the reddish glow of the lowering sun through the smoke, then back at Joseph. His handsome face was smudged with dirt and his eyes were narrowed and red. He noticed her looking at him.

"Are you all right, Sierra?"

She nodded, realizing that she had been staring at him.

He took her hand. "I'm sorry about Mrs. Evans." He lifted his head and looked past her. "I only hope Pa has the sense not to come looking for me—and that he keeps Camille in hand."

Sierra felt a smile touch the corners of her mouth. "You make her sound like a spirited horse."

Joseph nodded. "She is, in a way—a long-legged colt just learning to jump the gate."

"She's beautiful," Sierra said quietly, remembering with painful clarity the way she had felt, standing in the lobby watching Cameron as he watched Camille. She blushed, but if Joseph noticed in the hazy, late sunlight, he said nothing. Sierra put her hand in her coat pocket and felt the packet that held her father's prayer book and her mother's brush. Beneath it was Cameron's journal.

"Joseph," she said, and he turned from watching the smoke to look at her again. Without a word she pulled the journal from her coat and handed it to him. "Read it," she said.

The look of puzzlement on Joseph's face gave way to one of dark anger as he turned the pages. Sierra waited without speaking. Around them the sounds of the crowd rose and fell like waves. Someone jostled Sierra from behind, and she took a short step forward to keep her balance, her eyes still on Joseph.

"The man is a complete fraud," he said finally, closing the diary. "A con man."

She could only nod.

"What was he doing at your boardinghouse? Were you involved with him?" Joseph's eyes were narrowed and he was looking at her intently.

"No," Sierra said, but then she hesitated, remembering the day that Cameron had asked for her address. Why *had* he gone there? Joseph reached out to take her hand. The simple gesture felt so natural, so perfectly *right*, that she found herself pouring out her embarrassment, her foolish belief that Cameron had been attracted to her—her dreams of being cared for, loved, of being a gentleman's wife.

When she stopped talking, Joseph was tapping the cover of the journal with one finger.

Sierra looked up at the smoke-smeared sky again. It was getting dusky, partly from the smoke, partly because the day was waning. The crowd on the grassy slope was thickening. On all sides, people were talking in low voices.

"I am grateful you warned us, Sierra," he said with such earnest sincerity that she could only smile at him. He bent to kiss her forehead. "So will Pa, and Camille, if she will ever read it." He handed the journal back, a thoughtful expression on his face. "My sister might listen to you better than to either of us." He gestured and Sierra turned to look at the rising columns of smoke in the Mission district and beyond.

A shiver of fear went through her. "The fires are spreading so fast it seems impossible that anything will be left standing."

An older man with a long silver-gray moustache turned to look at her and nodded. His arm was tight around a small boy's shoulders. Beside them stood a girl of fifteen or so, her face bleak and weary. "There's no water," the man said slowly and deliberately.

His words were heavy and sad, and Sierra could only stare at him. "No water?"

"That's what I heard a fire captain say," the man told her. "The pipes were broken in the shakeup. There are the old cisterns here and there, but a lot of them are caved in, or weeds have grown over the lids and they can't find them at all."

Sierra blinked, watching the black plumes of smoke billowing upward to the east and north. She turned to scan the edges of the open field they stood in. People were still pouring in from the streets on the other side of Mission, standing shoulder to shoulder along the curbs. She noticed uniforms. There were so many soldiers. A sparkle of orange flame shot skyward, and the man who had spoken to Joseph nodded his head knowingly. "The gasworks."

"I don't think we should stay here," Joseph said, once the man had turned away again.

Sierra nodded. "The fires could come this way in the night."

He cupped her chin in his hand, lifting her head until she looked into his eyes. "If you want to go, we will," he whispered, leaning close into her ear. "We can start off up Laguna, then—"

"I know the streets and alleys better than you do," Sierra reminded him, their cheeks still touching. She could feel his smile even though she could not see it. He put his arms around her and held her tightly.

"You are the bravest woman I have ever known," he said softly. He held her closer. She felt her body fit against his as though they were puzzle pieces joined together at last. She closed her eyes. He hadn't told her she was beautiful, or charming, or delicate. He had said *brave*. She was so little that a woman was supposed to be, but that mattered less to him than her courage? She found herself leaning back to look at him and stared at his mouth, imagining what it would be like to kiss him with passion as well as love.

Joseph bent to brush his lips against hers. "Bigger is going to think you are wonderful," he said.

Sierra wanted to ask him who Bigger was, but at that moment the ground beneath their feet began to tremble, and they embraced again, holding each other as the crowd around them fell silent.

A sudden round of explosions compressed the air, hurting Sierra's ears. Only the sound of babies crying broke the sudden quiet.

Cameron bent close to whisper into Camille's ear. "It's too dangerous here." Gently he guided her forward, heading up Market Street, wondering if the trains were still running and if he could get to a station. There were flames in nearly every window, but, aside from coughing on the stinging smoke, people seemed not to notice. They stepped around the rubble and barely looked up when explosions came from down around the Mint Building.

A column of marching soldiers came onto Market from a side street and Cameron pulled Camille closer. The captain was shouting. Just then a few men leaped through the broken windows and began running, clutching boxes trailing ragged tissue paper in their arms.

Looters, Cameron thought, just as three shots rang out. The thieves scattered, each going a different direction.

"Where will we go?" Camille asked in a child's voice.

"Lafayette Square, I think," he told her. "It's open ground and a long way from the fire. We'll be safe there for the night. Tomorrow morning we can hire a carriage, and I will figure out how to get you home."

"My father will be indebted to you," Camille said. "And so will I." She looked at him with trusting eyes. He put his arm around her and she leaned into his side. Cameron kept his eyes moving, scanning the crowds in the streets, ready to change direction at a glimpse of Mr. Harlan or his son, thinking frantically, *This could all work out perfectly—even after everything that has gone wrong. Maybe the chambermaid won't tell Camille's brother anything. Why should she? Maybe she was in the process of trying to separate him from his wallet somehow. She didn't look or act like a con or a prostitute, but why else would he have been with her?*

Another thudding concussion shook the ground. Camille pressed close. "We have to hurry," he said as calmly as he could, unwrapping her arms from around his neck. He held her close to his side and got her walking again.

Ben Harlan was stunned listening to the Allmans' houseboy explain that Camille had run off. He clenched his fists, anguished at the idea of his daughter walking the streets alone. She would be scared—and prey to any rough-mannered fool who saw her.

Ben nodded dismissively and watched as the house-boy went back to his work of carrying paintings to the wine cellar. *How could the Allmans have left Camille? How could she have been so foolish as to run off?*

Damn that Slade, Ben thought, throwing a punch at thin air. *Damn him*. Camille would have gone with the Allmans if it hadn't been for him, Ben was sure. He looked up at the massive clouds of dark smoke rising from the city below and shook his head. Gerald Allman had been right to leave. One little shift in the wind and the flames would race uphill.

Suddenly Ben noticed a man riding one saddle horse and leading three more slowly through the rubble-littered street below the Allmans' house. His eyes narrowed, Ben began walking. Halfway down the hill, he reached inside his coat for his wallet.

Sierra's lungs were aching. The streets were getting less and less crowded as they went, and that worried her. The people whose homes had been ruined were finding places to spend the night. Every little vacant lot, every stretch of grass had a makeshift household set up upon it. A wind had risen, a strange direction-less flow of cool air dragged in by the rising of the fire's heat.

"Look at that," Joseph said, and his smoke-roughened voice was barely more than a whisper.

Sierra raised her eyes, blinking, trying to focus. She looked up Sacramento Street, past the wood-frame houses and shop fronts that sat like crooked blocks in a child's yard after the game is over for the day. Nothing looked remarkable—it was as damaged and awful as everything else they had walked past. She saw a gray-haired man sitting slumped over on the curb, crying silently. People were walking past, intent on their own problems.

Sierra looked wearily up at Joseph, not understanding.

"There," he said, pointing. "Tents."

Only then did Sierra pick out what he was talking about. Three or four blocks away she could just see a wide strip of dirty white canvas. At this distance, it looked more like sheets hanging on a long line, but as they got closer she saw that Joseph was right.

"Lafayette Park," she told him.

He nodded. "The army is probably setting up shelters in all the parks now."

Sierra nodded. It seemed to be true. There were even more soldiers in the park than they had seen elsewhere, and a long line of ragged, weary-looking people had formed in front of one of the tents. Joseph led her toward it without speaking. They fell in behind a broad-shouldered man and a heavyset woman, both crying almost soundlessly, sniffling and wiping at their noses with filthy handkerchiefs.

As she stood waiting with a hundred other people, Sierra felt the day's events settling onto her shoulders. The weight was almost more than she could bear. She could feel her mother's hairbrush in her pocket. In the distance she could hear the booming blasts they had been hearing off and on for hours. There wasn't going to be anything left of the city by morning.

"You will be able to rest soon," Joseph said softly and she felt his arm around her shoulders. Without meaning to, she leaned against him. There was a weariness settling into her body that was like nothing she had ever felt before. Mrs. Evan was dead. Sierra closed her eyes as the line moved forward. She let Joseph guide her two steps forward, then they stopped again. She did not open her eyes. They hurt so badly. It was as though the heat had burned them. Joseph nudged her forward another step.

With her eyes closed, Sierra began to notice the conversations around her. There was a couple behind them talking about whether or not they would be allowed to build fires to cook. The idea of *building* a fire seemed suddenly funny to Sierra, and she had to bite her lip to keep from laughing aloud. She was giddy and exhausted, and she knew it. Joseph tightened his arm around her shoulders and moved her forward again.

When Sierra finally opened her eyes, only the crying couple stood between them and the army officer. He handed the weeping man a piece of paper and gestured for him and his wife to move off.

"Just the two of you?" The soldier asked the question, then turned to shout at someone off to his right. When he looked back, Joseph nodded. "But I am looking for my sister."

"Your names are. . . . ?"

"Joseph and Camille Harlan," Joseph said. "And Sierra—" he hesitated and Sierra could see that he had forgotten her last name. She took a breath to speak, but the soldier was already thrusting a paper into Joseph's hands, his eyes flickering past them.

"Harlan. Good enough. Tent number 39." The soldier pointed. "If your sister shows up, I can direct her out to you."

Joseph tried to speak again, but the man gestured emphatically, waving them away. Sierra cleared her throat to speak up on her own behalf, but the soldier repeated his impatient gesture. "Next in line!"

Joseph put his arm around Sierra's shoulders, and they made their way uphill through the crowds. Sierra looked into the faces of the people standing in loose groups in front of the low canvas tents. Many of them looked pale, stunned. Sierra lowered her eyes, wondering if they were as saddened by her face as she was by theirs.

Joseph kept her moving, and she kept glancing at him sidelong, thinking. His wife. The soldier had assumed they were married. He had obviously been too tired and preoccupied to see the difference in how they were dressed. Joseph had no proper hat on, but his clothes were fine and new, a contrast from her shabby dress.

"Here," Joseph said. She turned to look at him. He was peeling his coat off, gesturing toward a tent. Sierra noticed for the first time that there were numbers painted on the canvas flaps. "Go on inside, Sierra."

She started to shake her head. Even though the dusk was deepening into evening and she was heavy with weariness, she could not imagine herself sleeping while the whole city burned down around them.

Joseph ducked into the tent, and she could hear him rummaging around. "There's a blanket," he announced. There was such happy surprise in his voice that Sierra could not help but smile a little. Lifting her sooty skirts, she bent over and stepped into the tent.

"Here," Joseph repeated.

Sierra couldn't see at all. The canvas blocked the last light of day. She reached out carefully and touched Joseph's face. He caught her hand and held it for a long heartbeat, then he pulled her toward him.

The tent was a musty, crooked affair, obviously hastily pitched. Its sloping canvas walls were only a foot from the next tent. Sierra could hear children crying somewhere close by. They sounded frightened and miserable.

She leaned against Joseph, grateful for the strength of his arms around her. He was still for so long that it surprised her when he kissed her the first time. The second time, she felt herself kissing him exactly as she had imagined, with passion as well as love.

14

Camille sat huddled, her arms around her knees, as the sun came up through the haze of smoke that hung over the city. Cameron was still asleep, stretched out on the cold hard ground as though it were the finest of beds. She had been alone with her spinning thoughts much of the night.

She stretched her cramped legs, wriggling her toes inside her blackened shoes. She wanted to go home, to the ranch, as quickly as she could. Her father would be out of his mind with worry, and so would Joseph. But Cameron wanted to go north by train, as soon as they could find an open station. He assured her it was best—that they would never be able to get safely back through the mobs of people trying to get to the ferry building. He also thought the city would soon be lawless and dangerous.

Camille was touched by his constant concern for her safety, by the way he'd kept her so close by his side as

166

they walked through the unending crowds. She sighed, looking at him in the grayish predawn light. He was terribly handsome. And he loved her.

She stood up silently to stretch her legs, brushing the loose grass and twigs from her skirt. It was ruined, torn along the hem and stained with soot and dust. Papa would not be happy about that, but what could she have done? She shook her head ruefully, knowing what Papa would say. She should have gone with the Allmans. But if she had, she was not sure that she would ever have seen Cameron again—and surely that was worth any upset from Papa.

Camille cleared her throat and winced at the sharp stinging of her smoke-raw lungs. She looked across the park. A few people were stirring. But not many. Perhaps the soldiers had water. The very idea that water might be close—might be had for the asking—was enough to make her throat ache with thirst. She lifted her dirty hemline and tiptoed away from Cameron. She would bring him water, too, if she could, and she would hurry, to be back before he awoke and found her gone.

Ben Harlan had not slept. His mouth tasted like ashes, and his left knee was aching badly. He had dozed lightly, one hand on his pistol, wary of anyone who came too close to his horses. He had bought all four—saddles and all—from the man who had been leading them and swore he was their rightful owner. Ben could only hope it was true and that he hadn't handed a horse thief good American money.

He had led the animals along the edge of the destroyed section of the city, skirting the fires, until he found some rope in a collapsed shed next to a burned-out grocery. He had taken exactly what he needed, asked after the name of the owner, and copied it carefully onto a scrap of paper he tucked into his waistcoat pocket. He would make good on the debt as soon as he was able.

Using the rope, Ben had tied the three spare horses together like pack mules, head to tail, single file, then had ridden in a relentless straight line back toward the fires. As long as there was daylight he had kept the horses moving, finding less crowded streets and riding a wide perimeter, making his way back to Market as often as he could to sit uneasily astride his nervous mount and search the faces coming past him.

The horses were flighty and dangerous, and Ben knew he had no business riding them into crowded streets—but he had no choice that he could see. They could only stand so much of the fire at a time, then he would have to let them trot away from it, their eyes rimmed in white. The explosions, which started down around the Mint and then pounded their way up along Van Ness, made things worse, scaring the endless crowds of people as well as his fidgeting mounts.

Ben understood perfectly what was happening. The firemen were dynamiting buildings along the edge of the blaze for the same reason a rancher would start a controlled backfire to stop an approaching wildfire. Van Ness was the widest street in the city next to Market. The firemen were trying to make the gap too wide for the conflagration to jump across it.

As the sun went down, Ben, tears stinging in his eyes, turned his mount around in a wide arc so that the other three could follow without tangling. By the time the dark had swallowed the city, he had found a vacant corner lot with trees and had claimed a spot along one edge where four trees grew close together. He had tethered his horses without anyone objecting. He had not even tried to lay down on the hard ground, but had propped himself up against a tree trunk and rested, letting himself doze lightly off and on.

Now, in the dusk before dawn, Ben rubbed at his painful knee, watching the sky lighten. There was an ugly red glow above the fires, as there had been most of the night, but it was fading as the sky brightened.

Slowly, bracing himself against the tree, Ben stood up. He worked out most of his kinks while he resaddled the horses and swung back up onto his horse. His only hope of finding Camille safe and sound was to do it quickly. Every hour that passed increased the chance that trouble would find her first. Joseph could fend for himself longer, perhaps indefinitely.

Ben rode onward, stopping only to ask a soldier what was being done for the refugees.

"The parks are being turned into camps, sir," the soldier answered politely and Ben saw that he was probably younger than Joseph underneath the soot and weariness on his face.

"Where's the closest?"

"Five blocks up, then left on Sacramento," the soldier told him. "There's three hundred tents, maybe more. They'll give you a place to rest."

Ben thanked the boy and rode on once more. When he got to the little park, he rode the perimeter slowly, peering at the murky shapes of people sprawled out on the grass, admitting to himself that he had to wait for more light before he gave up on the park. He could easily ride straight past his daughter in the gray predawn light, even if she was outside a tent where he could see her.

As Ben guided his mount off the grass and dirt, back onto the cobblestone street that bordered the little park, the horse threw up its head and tossed its mane, whinnying. A second later, the three tethered to its saddle were crowding up, their ears pricked forward.

An instant later, Ben understood why. Just ahead of him, a wagon loaded with thick-waisted oaken barrels stood beside a military tent. Men in uniforms were talking beside it as soldiers wrestled the barrels to the ground. Just past them, another soldier was using a crowbar to open the casks. As he lifted one of the round lids, Ben saw a silvery shine and heard what the horses had heard. The sound of water.

Sierra awoke and found that Joseph's arms were still around her. She remembered his touch and the amazing warmth of his mouth the night before and blushed. Only then did she remember the earthquake and the terrible fires. Wriggling gently from Joseph's embrace, she sat up and untangled her skirts, retying her belt.

Then she ducked down to peer from beneath the tent flap. The sky was graying, dawn was close.

Suddenly lonely without the sounds of the north-bound whistle and Mrs. Evans's rooster, she was caught in an aching memory of the boardinghouse that she had called home. Was it still there? Had it burned?

Sierra reached back into the tent to pull out her coat, then stepped out of the tent and straightened, putting it on. The packet of her parents' things in one pocket and Cameron's diary in the other greeted her hands as she shoved them inside to warm them. She took a few steps to see past the tents, and then—when she couldn't—a few more. There were people sleeping all over the grass. She blushed again, wondering if the soldier had sent someone to share the tent with them and they hadn't noticed, or had been asleep, entwined in each other's arms.

A little thrill of joy went through Sierra's body. Joseph had told her that he loved her, and she believed him with every bit of her heart. Then the thrill subsided into a shiver as she recalled what Joseph had said about his father probably not approving of her.

Sierra stood very still, and the morning cold gradually seeped into her heart. Joseph had also said that he would give up his father's blessing and his inheritance before he would risk losing her. She tried to believe that, too, but it was harder. Especially now, in the chill morning air, standing in a park crowded with refugees. Everyone was huddled together for warmth and comfort. Everyone was frightened. Maybe there were a thousand couples waking up this morning and wondering what love was really made of.

Sierra glanced back at the tent. Maybe she should run away right now. She could make her way alone. She always had. She felt her eyes sting and blinked back tears. Most likely he would make up some excuse to leave her here. Or, even if his intentions were good, he would acquiesce when his father objected to her. Sierra remembered all too well the day in the room at the Palace and how Ben had treated her. He was not going to want a chambermaid for a daughter-in-law.

Sierra pressed the back of her hand against her lips. She took a few steps without meaning to, as though she was edging away from the pain she imagined. It would almost be better to have a memory of a single, wonderful night and a dream of what might have been than to face the cold reality of losing Joseph.

Sierra looked down at her soiled, worn dress and all the glow of the night seemed to fade. Who was she trying to fool? Caught up in the danger of the earthquake and the fire, Joseph had clung to her, and imagined himself in love, but he would come to his senses soon enough. She would never believe that he had consciously taken advantage of her, but it would work out that way, nonetheless. She had given herself willingly, and refused to regret it. But she could spare herself the pain of the inevitable.

Sierra found herself walking without really meaning to, glancing back every few steps, promising herself that if he appeared in the opening of the tent now, she would turn and run back. But he didn't. She pulled in a deep breath as she made her way around a family sprawled inside a ring of trunks. A spaniel lying beside a blond-haired child lifted its head and snarled a low warning. Sierra kept going.

Camille asked three or four people if they had water to share and got regretful shrugs. She looked back toward Cameron's still form on the grass and decided to go a little farther. There were soldiers everywhere. No harm would come to her.

"Is there drinking water?" she asked the next soldier she passed. He stopped and gazed at her so long that she began to feel uncomfortable. She knew her hair was mussed and her skirt torn, but she looked no worse than anyone around her. Then she saw the little half smile on the man's mouth and blushed.

"Over there," he said finally. "You have family here?"

"Oh, yes," Camille said quickly. "My father and four brothers." She pointed back toward the crowded area where Cameron lay sleeping.

The soldier tipped his cap and gestured. "Right over there, Miss. See the draft team?"

Camille looked past him and noticed the beer wagon for the first time, unmistakable even in the early light because of its thick-spoked wheels and the sheer size of the team. It was full of barrels. She nodded her thanks and started toward it, her corset pinching as she walked. She felt dirty, and she longed to clean her teeth and comb her hair. She must look a perfect sight, and it bothered her, even though it was hardly her fault.

There was a line beginning to form near the wagon, and Camille stepped through the sleeping people more quickly, picking as careful a path as she was able. As she got closer, she could see the soldiers breaking open boxes and heard a clinking sound. She hoped they had tin one-pint growlers to carry water in, or cups at least. She wanted to waken Cameron with a drink of clean water. He had to be as thirsty as she was.

"Camille!"

She spun around at the sound of her father's voice. He had dismounted and was walking toward her, a pack train of horses filing behind him. He beamed at her, and held out his arms.

Without a single thought, she raced toward him, and when he swept her up into his arms she giggled like a child.

"Oh, thank God you're safe," he said against her hair. "Oh, thank God, thank God." He held her away for a second and scrutinized her face. "Are you all right? Has anyone harmed you?"

"Cameron has saved me any hurt," she said quickly and watched his face darken. "Papa, he has been perfectly proper and has only protected me."

"Do you know where your brother is?" he demanded, from beside the hindmost horse. She watched him untie it and walk it forward, extending the reins to her.

"Mount up. I couldn't find a sidesaddle, so mind your skirts." He reached out to touch her cheek.

"I don't want to leave Cameron here, Papa," she interrupted.

He shook his head, scowling. "He's a grown man, Camille. He can take care of himself."

"But I don't want to *leave* him," she repeated. All night, in spite of the flames and the fear, she had felt like a woman—like someone who had taken her fate into her own hands. Now, facing her father, she felt reduced to childhood by his immutable sternness.

"But you are going to," he was saying in a low, terse voice. "This is not a time to argue, Camille." He gripped her shoulder and guided her alongside the horse. "Let's go find your brother."

Angry and protesting, Camille let him give her a leg up. She settled into the saddle awkwardly. Though she had grown up riding astride, she had gotten used to the sidesaddle over the past four or five years. Pa had insisted it was ladylike, never mind the progressive women and suffragists who thought sidesaddles were death traps.

"There are four horses," she began again. "Cameron could just come with us back to the ranch and—"

"No!" Ben exploded. "Now be still and do as I say."

He turned his stirrup to mount; she could see his eyes flicker from her face to her reins, and she understood his intent. The instant he was mounted he was going to jerk her reins free. Then he would lead her horse, as if she really were a child.

Sierra had stopped looking back. Joseph was not going to awaken and call out her name. There would be no magical sign—it was up to her. And she was walking away, faster and faster, heading down the long slope. The sun was rising, blood red through the pall of smoke, and she could see pillars of black still billowing skyward over the city. Chinatown, she realized, had burned. She winced, imagining the intricate, crowded maze of wooden houses and shops on fire. It must have been terrifying.

Sierra stumbled over a suitcase someone had left lying on the ground, and scolded herself for being so oblivious of her footing. Regaining her balance, she allowed herself one glance back toward the tent. Joseph was still inside. . . . He had called her brave. But if she was, why was she running away now?

The question answered itself in her mind. Nothing stayed forever in her life. Nothing ever had. Every time she had felt loved and safe and secure, something had happened to throw her back into the world, alone. Joseph would most likely obey his father's wishes and marry someone of his own class.

Sierra nearly bumped into a gray-haired woman who was walking slowly, leading an elderly man along. They were carrying a little tin bucket like the ones the saloons gave out to steady customers. Sierra stared at it, her throat tightening at the sight of cool fresh water.

"There's a wagon down below, dear," the woman said in a friendly voice.

Sierra nodded, running her tongue over her lips. She would get a drink, then. It would give her time to think, time to decide whether she should run now, or risk the hurt she was virtually certain would come if she did not.

Ben Harlan was furious. Camille sat on her mount, looking down at him, her pretty face smudged with ashes and dirt. Her eyes were wild. The earthquake and the danger of the fire had gotten her overexcited, he was sure. Or something had. She had spent the night with that damn Slade, he was sure, and if the man had so much as touched her. . . .

"Papa?"

"Be still!" he shouted at her, unnerved by the directness of her gaze, the flash of reckless resolve he thought he saw in her eyes. She wasn't thinking clearly, wasn't *capable* of a considered decision, and it was his duty to keep her from making a foolish one.

He twisted the stirrup around, snapping the leather straight, measuring the distance between the loop of Camille's reins and his left hand. He would lead her out of here if it was the last thing he did. And he was going to shoot that blasted dandy if he ever saw him again.

Jamming his left foot into the stirrup, Ben leaned forward, reaching for the reins. But the grinding pain in his left knee startled him into crying out. Camille was jerking her mount around as Ben hit the ground shoulders first, his foot caught in the stirrup. He tried to call out to her, but she was already lashing at her horse with the ends of the reins, hell-bent on escape and completely unaware that he was in trouble.

"Whoa!" Ben shouted as Camille pounded off, her hair flying. His own horse was sidling, tossing its head. If it took off now, it would drag him and maybe kill him. "Whoa!" he repeated, not nearly as loudly as he had meant to. The pain in his knee was sharp, terrible. With his shoulders on the ground, Ben wrenched around, trying to regain his feet as his horse sidled and stamped. It reared, and for an eternal second he saw the heavy hooves above him, and he waited to die. Then someone grabbed the animal's trailing reins, hauling it down a little to one side.

Impossibly, Ben saw a young woman with wild dark hair step to the saddle. With an expert flip of the stirrup shoe, she freed his foot and he rolled clear, gasping at the stab of pain in his knee.

Then suddenly the girl was bending over him. "Mr. Harlan?" She backed the horse up, and he saw her glance at the other two to make sure they were standing steady before she spoke again. "Are you all right?"

"I will be," he grunted, fighting to stand. His leg bore his weight, even though it hurt like Hades. He reached out and grasped the rope of the closest of the two spare mounts and used it to keep his balance. Their heads were high but they were calm enough.

"Was that Camille?" The girl's voice startled him.

He nodded, staring at her. "And who the hell are you?"

She swung up onto his horse like a man, settling

into the saddle with ease and authority, ignoring the too-long stirrups in favor of her own practiced balance. She looked at him. "Joseph is in tent 39. I'll bring Camille back if I can. I'm the chambermaid."

Before he could react, she whirled the horse around and was urging it into a gallop, going in the direction Camille had taken.

❦ 15 ❧

Cameron woke and was startled to find Camille gone. He jumped up, expecting to see her close by. She had fawned on him all night long. Another kind of man would have taken advantage of her, he was sure. But he wasn't after the easy prize. He wanted the whole shooting match—the ranch, the life, the respect.

"Camille?" he called out. It was barely sunup. Where would she have gone? Then he realized what the answer must be. She had probably gone looking for a water closet to use. Had the soldiers set up some kind of latrine? They soon would, he was sure. They would have to.

Cameron scanned the faces he could see, then squinted into the distance. He wasn't sure whether to go looking for her or stay put so she could find him when she came back. The thought that her father would hardly respect such a passive attitude started him walking. His whole plan hinged on Ben Harlan being grateful for his honorable care of his daughter throughout this dangerous disaster.

Ten minutes later, Cameron began changing his plan. If Camille had been silly enough to leave the house of her father's friends, maybe she was silly enough to have wandered off again. The last thing he wanted to do was to have to admit to Ben Harlan that he had somehow lost his daughter. He clenched his fists, furious with her for ruining everything. He walked the park once more, end to end, and could not see her. Then, cursing, he started away, heading toward the train station, shaking his head. Damn the earthquake and the hell with silly girls. He would find an older woman next time—a wealthy widow. One with sense enough to appreciate his attentions and with money of her own.

"Joseph Harlan?"

Jerked into wakefulness by his father's voice, Joseph sat up and saw that Sierra was gone. Then he remembered the whole wonderful night, and the terror that had preceded it—all in one clashing instant.

"Joseph, answer me!"

"I'm here, Pa," he said, standing up and stepping out of the doorflap. His father was leading two horses, an expression on his face that Joseph had never seen before.

"Pa, are you all right?"

"It's my knee. Get me into this damn saddle. We have to find your sister." Joseph shook his head, trying to understand as his father launched into a staccato explanation of Camille's rebellious escape.

"But I have to find Sierra first, Pa," he interrupted, and saw his father's face darken.

"And who in blazes is Sierra? Some trollop you—"

"She was our chambermaid at the Palace," Joseph said curtly. "And I love her." He watched his father's face go through another unfamiliar change—somewhere between astonishment and fury.

"This chambermaid—can she ride?"

"Like a race-jockey," Joseph said, wondering why his father was wasting time on such a strange question, then remembered himself wanting to ask Sierra the same thing. He blinked. Nothing was making sense.

"Get me up. On the right side—my good leg," Pa ordered. "I know where they both are."

Joseph slung his father into the saddle awkwardly, then threw one stirrup over the saddle as he tightened the cinch on his mount. He mounted in one fluid motion. His father nodded and set his hat, and they rode cautiously through the crowds, letting the horses canter only once they were back on the road.

"You love her?" Pa asked over the sound of the hoofbeats as the sun burst over the horizon.

"Yes!" Joseph shouted, and saw his father grimace.

Sierra's horse was fleet-footed and agile, and she was grateful. Of course, a wealthy rancher like Ben would pick the best of the four to ride himself. As she maneuvered through the rubble and the uneven, damaged street, she could just see the flashing of Camille's white blouse up ahead. Camille rode expertly, Sierra could tell, weaving her horse in and out of the scattered crowds. She wasn't galloping flat out—that was impossible, with the streets full of overturned wagons and abandoned goods, and people walking like exhausted automatons—but she was keeping up as fast a pace as could be managed.

Sierra urged her horse onward, keeping Camille in sight as she turned up a wider street and then turned again, heading downhill. The farther they got from the tall brick buildings in the center of town, the clearer the streets became. The wooden structures here had skidded sideways on their foundations, but there were no bricks scattered in the roadway. And the fire had not yet come this far.

In one long, clear stretch that lasted about a half mile, Camille let her horse gallop, clattering along like a runaway. Sierra sat her horse carefully, keeping her balance centered high, over its shoulders, helping it as much as she could. She gained a little ground and wondered if Camille was even aware she was being pursued. She had not looked back once.

Camille pulled her horse into another wide, galloping turn, and Sierra followed, a little closer behind. She let her mount out again, but this time the horse didn't extend as fully—it was getting winded. Sierra patted her horse's sweaty shoulder and leaned back a little, allowing it to slow, to rest. It was enough to keep Camille in sight.

Camille made two more right-hand turns, taking a roundabout route that could lead eventually back to the park, Sierra realized. She was calming down, no doubt, and beginning to wonder what she should do next. Sierra just kept the gap between them from widening. She was a good half mile behind when Camille reined in abruptly, slowing her mount to a trot.

Sierra saw her chance to close the distance, so she leaned forward, urging her mount faster, reining to one side to miss a board with long iron nails projecting from it and then to the other, to avoid a smashed piano. She rode hard, expecting Camille to hear her horse's hoofbeats and look back, but she didn't.

"Camille!" Sierra shouted when she got close enough.

The girl wrenched around in her saddle, hair flying and eyes wide. She frowned, looking puzzled, as Sierra cantered alongside.

"Who are you?" Camille's eyes were full of genuine confusion. Sierra felt a strange hollowness inside herself. Joseph had told her about his father and sister, and of course they had never met her—not really—but the oddness of it still bothered her. How could it be that they had seen her as often as she had seen them, but had never once looked at her with enough interest to recall her face?

"Your father asked me to bring you back," Sierra said aloud. "He is hurt and—"

"Papa's hurt?" Camille interrupted.

"You didn't see because you had already turned, but he tried to mount and it was as though his leg just gave way. He fell, and—"

"His bad knee," Camille said, and there was such anguish in her voice that Sierra began to like her. "Is he all right?"

Sierra nodded. "He will be, I think. Are you?"

"He wants me to stop seeing Cameron and I . . ." Camille began, then she struck her fist against the pommel of the saddle. "And once Papa makes up his mind you can't argue with him, ever."

Sierra was acutely aware of the small weight in her coat pocket. She reached for the journal, careful not to pull her own small packet free as she drew it out. "You must read this."

Camille's eyes went wide. "Whatever for? I should get back to my father and—"

"He would want you to read it," Sierra assured her. She leaned out of her saddle and Camille reached to take the journal. "It's Cameron's," Sierra said, and watched Camille's eyes widen. "I stole it from his room to give to you. I was a chambermaid at the Palace Hotel before—all this." Sierra waved one hand at the damaged buildings along the street and the towering pillars of smoke to the east.

Camille opened her mouth to speak, but Sierra held up one hand. "Read it first."

Joseph had a hard time keeping up with his father. In spite of the awkward angle of his left leg in his stirrup, he pushed his horse as hard as anyone could have through the debris-littered streets.

Two soldiers had given them the general direction the girls had taken, but beyond that, they had no idea.

Joseph watched his father rein in over and over, slowing just enough to call out to passersby. Some seemed not to hear the question, others looked startled as they emerged timidly from their front doors and walked into the early sunlight. But every third or fourth time someone would nod and gesture, indicating the direction the girls had ridden.

The new day was stained with the color of the smoke, the odd, sifted light casting a ruddy film over everything, changing even the green of the trees slightly. Nothing looked quite *familiar*. Everywhere along the streets people were appearing, walking in slow circles around their homes, assessing damage, talking to their neighbors in low voices. They all kept glancing eastward, toward the fires.

"Have you seen two girls riding fast?" Pa called out to a group of men who had congregated on a corner. Joseph pulled his horse in as a tall fellow in a suitcoat pointed up a side street.

Following his father's lead, Joseph rounded the corner at a canter and felt his heart leap as he spotted two riders about a half mile up the road. They were still mounted but had stopped their horses. It looked like they were talking. One turned, and Joseph saw the dark cape of Sierra's long hair flare out from her shoulders.

"Come on," Pa said and leaned forward in his saddle, grunting with pain, about to urge his tired horse into a gallop.

"No, Pa. Wait."

Joseph leaned out to grasp his father's reins, slowing his own mount and his father's at the same time. He pulled both animals to a halt and heard his father curse. "Let them talk, Pa. I think it could be important."

Ben spat, leaning to the side, then straightened, frowning. "And would you mind telling me what a chambermaid has to say to my daughter that could be so important this morning?"

"I would rather not, Pa," Joseph said evenly.

He watched as his father's exasperated expression changed slowly to an angry scowl. Joseph let the silence between them deepen. He knew Pa resented this—but if he found out what a scoundrel Slade really was, poor Camille would never hear the end of it. Joseph exchanged a glance with his father, then looked back at the girls in the distance. They were still stopped, leaning sideways in their saddles, their heads close together.

Joseph let go of his father's reins and nudged his own horse into a sedate walk, relieved when Pa matched the slow pace.

"I have something else to tell you, Pa," Joseph began. "This might not be a good time, but—"

"It isn't," his father interrupted brusquely.

"I'm going to marry her."

Joseph waited while his father reined in, stared at him, then put his horse back into an ambling walk. "She is beautiful, in a wild way."

"She's much more than that," Joseph said.

His father didn't answer for so long that they were almost within shouting distance of Sierra and Camille before he spoke. When he did answer, it was short and to the point. "All right, then."

Joseph resisted the urge to whoop aloud. He managed to nod respectfully. "You won't be sorry, Pa."

"You might."

"Never, Pa."

"I am going to rewrite my will. No part of the ranch will ever be yours. Everything will go to Camille—and to whatever proper husband I can find her."

Joseph turned to look at his father, swallowing hard. He had dreamed of running the ranch as long as he could remember. "You don't mean that."

"I do."

Joseph stared at his father's angular profile. He had been prepared for anger, for an argument—not for this cold announcement, and it shocked him into silence. But he squared his shoulders. If the choice was the ranch or Sierra, he would find a way to build his own damn ranch. Sierra would help him, work alongside him, the way his mother had worked alongside Pa. He pressed his lips into a grim line and rode on in silence.

Sierra spotted them first. She leaned toward Camille, who was still turning the pages of the journal, her face streaked with tears. "Your father and Joseph are coming."

"Oh, no!" Camille whispered, reaching up to wipe the wet from her cheeks. She shoved the journal back at Sierra, glancing sidelong up the road. "Hide it, please. Destroy it. If Pa ever sees it—"

"I will burn it first chance I have," Sierra reassured her. "I did show Joseph."

Camille nodded, sniffling. "He won't tell Papa." She turned to swipe again at her face, streaking the soot and dirt.

Sierra looked up to see Joseph smiling at her as he rode closer—and a grim, ugly expression on Ben Harlan's face. His left leg was held oddly straight, the stirrup jutting outward. He was obviously in pain . . . but it was more than that.

"Can you tell I was crying?" Camille whispered.

Sierra lowered her chin and spoke from the side of her mouth. "Yes. Over your father being hurt."

Camille flashed her a grateful glance, then turned her horse to face her father as he rode up. "Papa, I am so sorry. I didn't see you fall. I didn't know—"

"I'll be all right," Mr. Harlan interrupted her. Sierra was caught staring at his angry face, as his eyes flickered past Camille to meet her own. "I have told my son that he can marry whatever chambermaid of no fortune or family he wishes, so long as he understands that it means giving up his inheritance and leaving the ranch forever."

Sierra drew in a painful breath and looked at Joseph, her heart constricting. "You can't do that. The ranch is everything to you!" She felt tears springing into her eyes.

"*You* are everything to me," Joseph said, riding close enough to touch her cheek. "We can build our own place somewhere."

"Let's get going, then, Camille," Ben said sharply. "I

want to go to the Palace if we can get there. Maybe something can be salvaged from your trunks, if there have been guards and everything isn't burned up or stolen by now." He paused. "Joseph? Will you come back with us to get your things?"

Sierra glanced at Ben Harlan. He was looking back and forth between Joseph and Camille, his eyes skipping across her as though she were invisible now.

Camille rode off to one side all the way back to the Palace Hotel. She tried to smile a little at her brother and Sierra, glad they hadn't just ridden off by themselves—though that seemed to be exactly what Papa had wanted them to do. It was obvious they were in love and happier than any pair she had ever seen, and she was glad for them. But her own heart was broken and uncertain, and her mind reeled with questions. How could she have so misjudged Cameron? Was she really like all the girls Joseph despised, shallow and silly? What had Cameron thought when he woke up alone and she was not there? Had he even cared?

"Keep up, Camille," Papa shouted, and she pressed her heels into her mount's sides, speeding up. Papa was making a trail boss's gesture, a rolling motion with one hand that meant she was to ride beside him. She sighed and obeyed.

"What do you think of her?" He jutted his chin at Sierra and Joseph, riding a ways ahead, riding close together.

Camille arched her brows. "You're asking *my* opinion?"

He nodded curtly. "I am."

Camille smiled, her heart a little lighter. "I think she is kind and good-hearted and can ride as well as any Harlan ever rode—including you."

"Bigger would like her, you think?"

"Bigger will love her, especially if she can cook."

"Can she?"

Camille laughed. "Papa, I don't know."

He nodded. "If she can't we could hire Sarah Mason and save her from that wretch she married once and for all." He paused. "If she made it through all this." He took a deep breath, then fell back into silence as they wove their way into the desolate streets south of Market, where the fire had come and gone. Camille stayed beside him, partly so that she could keep glancing at him instead of at the poor dead horses and the people sitting in despair on the curbs.

There were still flames in places among the blackened boards and fallen chimneys. but the worst of the fire was north of them now. An ambulance rattled past, spooking the horses, and Camille said a prayer for whoever was inside.

As he led his daughter up Montgomery Street toward Market, Ben Harlan saw what he had been afraid he would see. The Palace had been completely burned out. Maybe there would be an insurance settlement later, maybe not. For now at least, he was out seven or eight thousand dollars in fancy clothes for Camille, a fifth of that for Joseph and himself, his favorite stand-up hat, a pair of good boots, and his own trunk and suitcase—as well as the new trunks he had bought to hold Camille's clothing.

"I don't know that we can afford to come to town again anytime soon," he told Camille. Her head was tipped back. She was looking at the blackened stone, the rows of broken bay windows overhead.

"I don't care, Papa," she answered. "I am just grateful that none of us got hurt. And that Joseph found his love, Papa," she added, gesturing past the fallen stone and bricks to where Joseph and Sierra stood beside their horses. He was holding both their reins, and they were talking in low voices. As she watched, Camille saw Joseph drop down upon one knee.

Papa sighed, loud and long. Then he shook his head. "Well, the hell with it then."

Sierra had sat transfixed, staring into Joseph's eyes while he told her he loved her for the tenth time. She had been counting, and now she was sure he meant it. For the first time in her life, she was certain of something. Joseph loved her. He was willing to give up everything he had assumed about his life and future for her. She leaned toward him, and he embraced her. Then he waited for her to steady herself before he let go and knelt in front of her. "Will you marry me then?" he whispered.

"Yes," she whispered back. "Oh, yes."

"Will you come back to the ranch with us to get my things? If Pa will let us, I would like to get married there. But after that, we can go wherever you like."

Sierra pulled him to his feet and put her arms around him, swaying as he held her. "I have nowhere to go." She shivered, thinking about the boardinghouse—and the pile of ash and ruin that had taken its place. Poor Mrs. Evans. She had made it through so many things in her life, why not this one too? Sierra felt her eyes fill with tears.

At that moment, Ben Harlan turned his horse around. He rode toward them with such purpose in his eyes that Sierra fought back her tears and struggled against an urge to run. But when he got closer, she realized that he didn't really look angry anymore. He looked uneasy.

"Was that a proposal?" he demanded.

Joseph nodded and smiled. "And she said yes."

"Will you have the wedding at the ranch?"

Joseph narrowed his eyes. "That's what I want."

"I would be honored to be married where you and your wife were married, sir," Sierra said, watching his eyes. She couldn't tell what was on his mind, and she could only hope that he wouldn't say no now, just to deny his blessing and hurt Joseph even more.

Ben Harlan was silent for nearly a minute. Sierra could hear shouts from inside the gutted lower floors of the Palace. Behind her, the clipped rhythm of hooves on the cobblestones rose and fell again.

"So would an inheritance be an appropriate wedding gift?" Mr. Harlan smiled, a crooked, tentative smile.

"Hardly," Camille said from behind him. They all

looked up at her, startled. "That was always his, Papa, and you know he has earned it."

Ben Harlan shrugged, smiling up at his daughter. "I suppose you're right. I will have to think of something else."

Joseph turned and caught Sierra up in his arms, kissing her mouth. Then he released her to embrace his father. Sierra watched them step apart, still looking at each other, still smiling warily.

"I apologize," Mr. Harlan said.

Joseph's face was grave. "And I accept."

A silence came between them, stretching out until it was brittle and awkward.

"Joseph has talked a lot about the ranch," Sierra said timidly. They all turned to face her. "I can't wait to see it," she finished, feeling her cheeks heat up.

"Then we should get started," Mr. Harlan said. "I've had about all the excitement of city life I can stand for a while. How about you, Sierra?"

"I agree completely, sir," she answered with a straight face.

Joseph laughed aloud as he gave Sierra a leg up onto her horse, then helped his father mount. Camille winked at Sierra, then covered her mouth with a soot-smudged hand, her eyes dancing. Ben Harlan turned his horse, and they followed him down Market Street toward the ferry.

"I love you," Joseph whispered as the bay appeared before them, glittering in the morning sun. Sierra reached out. He took her hand, and they rode close enough so that their knees touched, all the way to the edge of the glittering water. He pointed across it. "I can't wait to get you home."

Sierra smiled, then turned her head to hide her tears as they took their places in the line of people waiting for the ferry. The sun was warm. Overhead, gulls wheeled in circles across the blue sky, far beyond the haze of smoke.

About the Author

KATHLEEN DUEY has written more than twenty-five historical novels for kids and young adults, as well as other kinds of books. She lives in a happy old house with the man she loves and has two sons who are suddenly much taller than she is. She is passionate about writing and researching her books, and has a great deal of fun doing it.